ALSO BY DAVID TRUEBA

Learning to Lose

Blitz

DAVID TRUEBA

TRANSLATED FROM THE SPANISH BY

John Cullen

OTHER PRESS | NEW YORK

Production editor: Yvonne E. Cárdenas
Text designer: Julie Fry
This book was set in Garamond with Futura.

10 9 8 7 6 5 4 3 2 1

Library of Congress Cataloging-in-Publication Data

Names: Trueba, David, 1969– author. | Cullen, John, 1942– translator.
Title: Blitz / David Trueba ; translated by John Cullen.
Other titles: Blitz. English
Description: New York : Other Press, [2016] | Description based on print
    version record and CIP data provided by publisher; resource not viewed.
Identifiers: LCCN 2016020381 (print) | LCCN 2016008311 (ebook) |
    ISBN 9781590517857 (ebook) | ISBN 9781590517840 (softcover)
Subjects: LCSH: Landscape architects—Fiction. | Spaniards—Germany—
    Fiction. | Munich (Germany) | BISAC: FICTION / Literary.
Classification: LCC PQ6670.R77 (print) | LCC PQ6670.R77 B5513 2016
    (ebook) | DDC 863/.64—dc23
LC record available at https://lccn.loc.gov/2016020381

For my brother Jesús,
with whom I've always shared a room

As Lightning to the Children eased
With explanation kind
The truth must dazzle gradually
Or every man be blind –

EMILY DICKINSON (c. 1872)

JANUARY

The message read:

haven't told him yet, it's really hard. argh. i ♥ u.

But the message wasn't for me. Life changes when the love messages aren't for you. That love message arrived like a lightning bolt, unexpected and electric, and changed my life.

I was standing at the bar, my fingertips brushing the green plastic tray on which a bustling cook would place my order as soon as it was properly embalmed in silver foil. I felt my cell phone vibrate in my pocket. I've never picked a sound to alert me to incoming calls or text messages. Ringtones are a nuisance, so sudden and rude. I don't even ring doorbells. If I can, I limit myself to a few little raps with my knuckles on the wood. So when it comes to my cell phone, the vibration's enough for me. Sometimes I'm afflicted with what's called vibrating phone syndrome, the false impression that your phone's vibrating in your pocket, and when you take it out you find there's no call, there's no message, it was all in your head. My friend Carlos says cell phones will have the same fate as cigarettes: seventy years after being popularized and diffused throughout the population, they'll come to be persecuted as a harmful addiction. He says there will be deaths, million-dollar judgments, and detox clinics. He says mobile phones affect the vital organs, and if you keep a phone in your pocket, every time you get a call the spermatozoa in your testicles undergo something like an electric shock. That's the reason why there are so many hyperactive children these days, he says. If my friend Carlos had been there with me at that moment, he would have said, you see? You see how much harm cell phones do? Because the vibration was real and the message came to me, even though I wasn't the person it was intended for. Marta had sent it. So I turned and looked over to where she was sitting, at the table next to the window. The table we'd sat down at just a very short while ago, before my life changed.

Marta and I had arrived in Munich the previous day. We didn't know the city, but a volunteer from the conference was waiting to drive us to the InterContinental hotel. She was holding a little card with my name on it, and she greeted us when we responded. I'm Helga, she said, introducing herself. We followed her to the parking area, where she gave us a little acrylic book bag with the schedule of events and our conference credentials. LEBENSGÄRTEN 2015, all the logos announced. There was a friendly welcome, printed in two languages, from the organizers, and another page giving the time of our presentation on the following day, the name of the contact person, and the sector in the convention center where the presentation would take place. For anything else, you can just ask me, the woman said. And during the drive to the InterContinental hotel, apart from a few questions about our trip, she kept quiet and let us look out the window and take in our surroundings with our own eyes. When the soccer stadium came into view, she pointed it out and said it was very famous for its architecture. I made some remark to Marta about the architects, but she didn't seem very interested.

The name of the conference, *Lebensgärten*, could be translated as "Gardens of Life" or "Life and Garden," although that last one sounded more like a magazine for middle-aged women. We'd been invited to the conference to present a project in competition with others. My work's hard for me to explain. For my demonstration on the following day, I'd show a series of computer-generated images that would save a good deal of explanation. The category we were competing in was "Future Prospects," which in German — *Zukunftsperspektiven* — sounded less empty and more metallic, more reinforced. This was an international competition, more than twenty projects were entered, and the prize was ten thousand euros. The challenge was to depict a landscape intervention, not necessarily a feasible or reasonable one; it was to be something like a fantasy or a fiction. A story competition, but instead of telling stories, we'd tell a garden. In our line of work, you get used to dreaming up impossible prospects, sidestepping the lack of funding or interest by realizing your vision in digital simulations.

My idea was a park for adults. An exterior urban space, simple and realistic. With benches for reading or taking a quick break from the office routine. As its main innovation, the park contained a forest of human-sized hourglasses, also known as sand clocks, which if you turned them over accorded you a measured period of time to devote to your own thoughts.

An hourglass could serve as a reminder and quantifier of time, but also as an escape. What I like about hourglasses is that they reformulate the notion of anxiety at time's passage; they transform this inevitable process into something visual. Actually, those were the words I planned to use in my presentation the next day. I thought I'd limit myself to saying that I like hourglasses, and that I like them because they illustrate the real meaning of life, namely submission to the law of gravity, like the sand that falls from the upper glass vessel to the lower one. The idea of the garden was that it would teach you to appreciate exactly what three minutes were. That's the way my

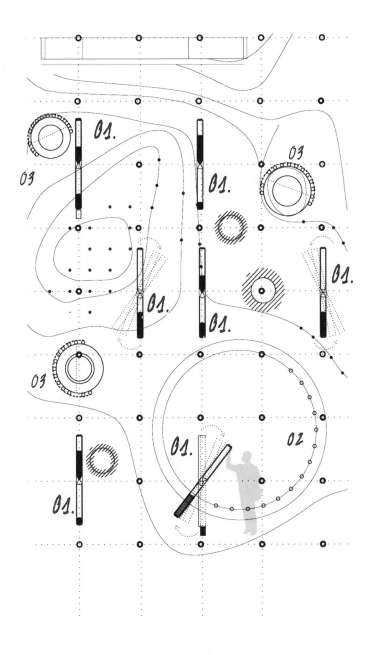

Idea of 'losing yourself' in another
SPACE - TIME

03.

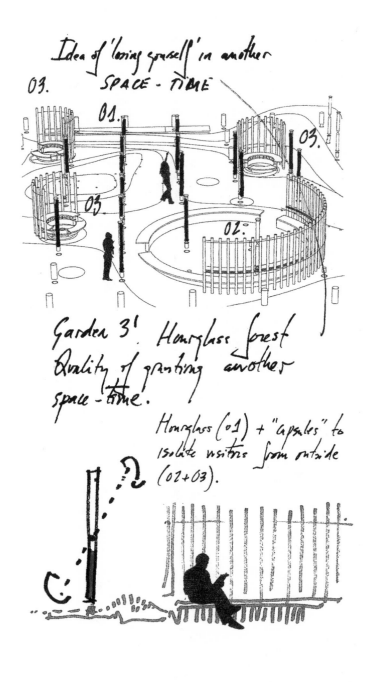

01.

03.

03.

02.

Garden 3'. Hourglass forest
Quality of granting another
space - time.

Hourglass (01) + "capsules" to
isolate visitors from outside
(02+03).

talk began: Has anyone here ever happened to stop and think about what three minutes really are?

I was more surprised than anyone when my "Three-Minute Garden"—or, as it was officially called, *Drei-Minuten-Garten*—was selected among the finalists. Along with the EURAU symposium and the IFLA world congress, the Munich conference was one of the most prestigious events in the world of landscape architecture. And over the course of the past ten years, the young prizewinners' projects had offered some outstanding, revolutionary ideas. As with all competitions, the mere fact that they'd accepted me as a contestant discredited the event somewhat in my view. Unemployed as we were in the midst of the economic crisis, our commissions few and far between, and resigned as we were to hibernation on a website that provided zero income, we were inclined to look upon contests as offering the possibility, however slim, of making some money. Marta and I were the only partners in our firm; we worked in a room in our apartment we called the office. Marta had studied neither architecture nor landscaping, but she was a person of rare sensitivity, always coming up with advice or corrections that improved my proposals. Working together extended our synchronicity as a couple, and we never quarreled. She was our company's administrator and representative. Nothing had been planned, because the business was originally an architects' studio five of us had founded after graduating from university. But little by little, the firm broke up and collapsed. The last to go was Carlos, when he accepted an offer from a more established architect. It seemed natural that Marta would join me in a last-gasp effort to stay afloat, in the days when I still cherished some hope that we could earn a living in such a flimsy profession.

I was nervous about my presentation. We'd already participated in several competitions, but we'd never been invited to a city to show our work in person. In almost every case, a letter would arrive informing us that our project had been short-listed, followed some time later by the news that another finalist had won. So Munich was a challenge. In fifteen minutes, and in English, we had to present our proposal to the panel of judges and the people in the audience. I was sure my absurd project had no possibility of winning; I figured the ultimate reaction to it would be sarcasm, and it would be dismissed as mildly amusing nonsense fitter for a playground than for advancing the career of a creator of public spaces. Marta calmed me down. Everything will be all right, she kept telling me, you'll see, and during that first day in the city she was affectionate and considerate with me.

Shortly after arriving, we visited the Gasteig cultural center and checked out the succinct montage of color photographs showing the various contestants and their work. Marta thought our project had a real chance to win. I thought we augmented the general mediocrity of the finalists. There was a park made out of garbage, an aquatic garden, an artists' corner with plastic figures, a children's recreational space. All this one needs is a plaster gnome, I grumbled. Marta hit me on the arm and looked around, hoping nobody had heard my disparaging comment.

At night I wanted to make love. Our double bed had two separate duvets instead of one big one we could share. A practical breakthrough, it turned out. And what a good idea: the couple don't steal each other's covers, and each can settle on his or her ideal temperature for sleeping. That rationality, which I identified with the German character, was what terrified me when I thought about my presentation the following day. My proposal was playful, almost frivolous, more emotional than scientific.

Marta didn't want to make love. She was tired from the long walk we'd taken through the snowy city, and her knees were hurting her. Her efforts to keep from slipping had put too much stress on joints weakened by years of ballet. Marta had stopped dancing at the age of twenty and turned to acting. She'd danced ever since childhood, but she'd eventually grown jaded and dissatisfied with her professional progress. She still had a dancer's body—powerful legs and beautifully smooth, harmonious musculature— flawed only by her feet, which lengthy practice sessions had hardened and slightly deformed, leaving her with crooked little toes and bunions from hours spent *sur les pointes*. Marta was ashamed of her ballerina's feet, and even when I applied myself to kissing and licking them she'd sometimes stop me with a nervous kick. On one occasion, she split my lip, but she consoled me so tenderly and delicately that I would have let her split my lip every night.

The life of an actress hadn't been any better for her. There were classes and then more classes; there were a few little roles in short films and stage plays seen only by her classmates and those of us who were her closest friends. She started thinking her true vocation was to be a student and take courses, but then she worked in a short film called *Los peligros de la conga*, "The Dangers of the Conga," which won prizes at various festivals and got nominated for a Goya. The film was an interesting, surrealistic story about a guy who goes to a wedding and returns home with a lady clinging to his belt. This lady, apparently the bride's aunt by blood, had latched on to him in a long conga line—almost all the guests had joined it—and she'd never let him go. Marta played the young man's girlfriend and housemate, and the arrival of this woman attached to her boyfriend's belt made her life impractical and difficult and threatened to end their living together until, after several weeks, they hit on a method of getting rid of the unwanted guest. They just needed to go to another wedding, and when the time came to dance the conga, the aunt would grab hold of someone else's belt.

Marta's part in *Los peligros de la conga* was the least interesting of the three. Her character was the only one who behaved with common sense, but the short got plenty of hearty laughs and loud applause, especially in the scenes when the three protagonists were in bed together, and for a few months Marta thought it would elevate her to some more ambitious projects. But they never materialized, and without making any open declaration, she quit acting, enrolled in correspondence courses in psychology, and began to work with me in my landscape architect studio, which was between the living room and the kitchen in our apartment. We complemented each other and coped with poverty while she insisted that I mustn't give up my vocation, my profession. I've already given up my dreams, and it's enough for one of us to do that, she'd say on the days when I let my discouragement show.

Marta had just turned twenty-seven, and she maintained that the number 7 was a serious, solemn number, always a decisive point in the decimal scale. She tried to convince me that in each decade, the 7 is more end than beginning, more like a terminal station. Seven is the age of reason. At seventeen, you're considered an adult. Twenty-seven is the end of youth. At thirty-seven, you indisputably enter the world of maturity. And that was the way Marta, with comic desperation, played the 7 scale. There are seven days in a week, the world was created in seven days, seven are the plagues of the Apocalypse. The 7

is a 1 obliged to lift its head, grow, and get older, as depicted in a drawing she dashed off on a paper napkin, where a good punch forces a number 1 to turn into a number 7.

I was three years older than she was, and I had more than enough reasons to cite the traumas of my thirty years. At my age, I had yet to find a paying job or a stable situation. I was adamant that Marta should understand how much longer youth lasted nowadays. Don't you see that we live to be ninety? Proportionately speaking, that means we're young until we're forty-seven or fifty-seven. Don't you see it in the street? Before, it used to be that only children wore sweat suits, I pointed out, but now they make them for all ages.

I thought Marta didn't want to make love because she was still angry at me. When we got back to the hotel, I'd tramped across the wall-to-wall carpet in our room with my boots on, leaving wet footprints and melting snow. Why wouldn't it occur to you to take your boots off before you got everything all wet? she complained, pointing at the little puddles on the carpet. I tried to turn it into a joke. Whose idea was it to put wall-to-wall carpet in a hotel room? I think it's disgusting to walk on a carpet a thousand other people have walked on before me. There's something dingy about it. It's like bathing in the previous guest's bathwater. Look, here are some traces left by a guy who jerked off in this room three months ago, and there's a wine stain, or maybe a bloodstain from a girl who was having her period the weekend before last, and look, look, can you see the little bitty guy waving over there, he's stuck, you see him? He's been forced to live in the carpet, hello, Herr Muller, shall I order you some dinner, or do you have enough with the breakfast crumbs left by the last several guests? Oh, excuse me, I don't mean to interrupt your cockroach training session. But Marta wasn't laughing at my obnoxious comedy routine and didn't think talking to the tiny creatures hiding in the shag carpet forest was funny.

I preferred not to insist on making love, which we hadn't been doing very much lately anyway. When we'd met five years ago, Marta was shattered and full of rancor. She'd broken up with a Uruguayan singer-songwriter, an arrogant guy despite his small-scale success, who left her for another girl he'd met during a tour as the warmup act for Jorge Drexler. His songs never interested me, but all Marta had to do was hear a chord in some bar or on the radio and her face would cloud over. I found it exciting, that sadness of hers, that private sorrow she never shared with anyone, and healing Marta's secret scar became for me a vital mission. We fucked without stint, but sometimes, all of a sudden, she'd start to cry. Making Marta laugh was my greatest pleasure in life. I'd exaggerate my clownish side, I'd act the comedian for all I was worth, and in the end she'd burst out laughing. Marta thought I was funny; she even thought my work—gardening—was funny, she told me. Marta's laughter was my reward. But lately Marta and I had been laughing less, and fucking less too. My friend Carlos said that was normal. For all intents and purposes, you're married, he said, you've been living together for more than four years, and married couples hardly fuck at all. You don't fuck the person you live with very often, just like you don't use soap every morning to wash out your coffee cup when you're the only one who drinks from it.

That first night in Munich we slept late, even without the sedative of sex. We had the unplugged feeling you get when you're far from home. Every now and then, her leg broke through the duvet barrier and brushed against mine. And after we ate breakfast in bed, we put the trays aside and took a nap. At my urging, which I thought subtle and affectionate, Marta gave me a hand job, and ejaculation always makes me sleepy, like a fat baby that's just been fed. When I woke up again, she was just emerging from the shower, glowing and beautiful, with her soaked hair dripping onto her powerful shoulders, more like a swimmer's than a ballerina's. I'm going to take a walk, she told me, and then I'll wait for you downstairs.

I showered for a long time, the pounding water as hot as I could stand, the steam enveloping me. When you don't stay in hotels very often, you tend to exploit their amenities. The water in our apartment in Madrid was under negligible pressure and came out tepid and dribbling, like an angel's pee. Actually, the apartment was Marta's, but I'd moved in with her when she gave up the dream of earning her living as an actress, and it was cheaper to share one rent. The financial crisis had accustomed us all to a pretty ridiculous level of insecurity, in that we accepted degrading jobs and subhuman salaries in order to feel we were still stakeholders in the system and not yet reduced to beggary. She considered herself the dispensable part of the business, but I needed her advice, her involvement, her eyes, whose vision extended beyond technical matters and revisions to plans. Participating in the conference and the competition in Munich was one of the few satisfactions afforded us by our work, which was an experiment on the verge of failure.

The next work we're going to consider comes from Spain. That's how I was introduced by Helga, the same woman who'd picked us up at the airport and who greeted us with delighted familiarity when she saw us enter the Gasteig. She'd act as my German interpreter, she explained, in case somebody in the audience had trouble understanding my English. I assure you, *I* have trouble understanding my English, I admitted. And she laughed, showing a row of strong white teeth behind her barely painted lips. Helga moved between her native language and English easily and naturally when she introduced us to the conference director, a rather eccentric German whose eyeglasses hung from a little cord and who was stooped like the villain in an expressionist movie. Helga warned me that the director was a pretty complicated character: everybody says he's crazy, she said, but he's very talented. Two wonderful parks in Munich were preserved through his efforts, and he's very highly regarded in the city, she explained. And then she led Marta and me to the little auditorium where the presentations were to take place. Marta sat at the computer she'd use to project images onto a screen behind us. In the seats reserved for the jury, I saw some faces that looked as friendly as welcome mats. Some of the other contestants, easily identifiable by their suspicious, bored expressions, were also out there, along with the rest of the audience, a miscellaneous handful of curious and idle spectators. Helga spoke my name into the microphone and turned to me with a gesture indicating that the floor was mine. From the moment we stepped into the convention center, I'd received so many urgent reminders from people connected with the conference about the absolute necessity of limiting my presentation to the allotted fifteen minutes that I thought it would be appropriate to begin with this detail.

Everybody has asked me not to go over my fifteen-- minute limit, I said. Figuring in the time required for the German translation, I calculate that I have seven and a half minutes left to present my proposal. If we further subtract this preliminary statement and the conclusion, let's say I have three minutes. I paused at this turning point to let Helga translate. Then I went on: and that's precisely what my work is about. It's about the rush. The rush we live in. The rush. Helga translated *rush* as *Eile*. When Marta, whose English was way better than mine, revised my text, she'd chosen the word *hurry*, which to my surprised ears sounded like *Harry. Dirty Hurry*?

My garden is an attempt to give our time its true value back, to make us reflect on how we dispose of our time. I noticed the conference director in the audience, taking notes and looking interested in what I was saying. And so, I went on, I call my project "The Three-Minute Garden." *Der Drei-Minuten-Garten*, Helga repeated, with a pleased, encouraging smile. She was a mature woman, a little over sixty. Her good cheer and friendliness seemed unforced. She looked at me again, with genuine curiosity, and her interest calmed me down and made me feel confident about the images I was about to present. Marta smiled at me from her position at the computer, the lights in the room gradually dimmed, and a swift movement of her slender fingers threw the first image onto the screen.

I noticed several smiles when the forest of sand clocks appeared, followed by a simulated walk through it. I continued to explain the project and ended with an overview of the whole.

During the question period—all the questions were friendly and indulgent—the conference director intervened and asked something in German. Helga translated it for me in a very low voice, speaking very close to my ear. What did you want to say with your proposal, and to what degree do you consider it particularly Spanish? I smiled. I don't believe Spanish clocks measure time any differently from German ones, although judging from our very different

retirement plans, one might think so. I do believe that the reality of time varies according to each circumstance and each person. I paused now and then as I spoke to let Helga translate. It's not so much a question of what I wanted to say with my proposal as of what I'd like people in this place to feel. Consequently, instead of giving you my responses, I'd much prefer to hear yours.

Once we were offstage, I thought I'd acted too cocky. Marta disagreed and calmed me down. Helga offered congratulations and assured me that everyone had followed my exposition with great attention. I didn't seem too cocky? Ah, no, no, absolutely not. And the joke about retirement pensions, that didn't bother anyone? No, no. The next contestant was a landscaper from Denmark whose advanced age made me sad. Who knew, maybe I'd spend my life going from competition to competition without ever seeing my ideas realized, consoled by the potential conferences have and called a young landscape architect until I became a senior citizen. Are you going to take part in the creators' discussion panel tomorrow? Helga asked me in an aside. No, we're leaving tomorrow morning. I didn't want to add a day to our trip. I couldn't be bothered with those vacuous roundtables, which tended to be dominated by the most conceited person present. And besides, one of the participants was Alex Ripollés, who was something like my closest enemy in competitions, who had already beaten me on two occasions with other projects, and whose clever landscaping proposals always struck me as pretentious stylistic exercises that found favor with the judges. Marta didn't want to stay too long in Munich either, and later I recalled something she'd said in passing: I'd rather not stay long, I have too much to do at home. I didn't ask her any questions—too wrapped up in myself and my presentation, I'm afraid.

When we left the little auditorium, we said good--bye to Helga, who was dashing off to the airport to pick up another guest. He's Spanish too, do you know him? she asked, and tried to pronounce the name Alex Ripollés, but to my ears it sounded more like Alex *Gilipollez*, Alex Bullshit, which didn't suit him badly at all. I've never met him in person, not that I want to, I said, and Helga couldn't figure out whether I was joking or my uncertain English was playing tricks on me. After attending a couple of presentations, we escaped, and at the door of the conference hall I looked at the information board, which displayed the location and time of each contestant's appearance. Through an error, instead of writing *paisajista*, landscaper, after my name, they'd written *pajista*, wanker. Beto Sanz, wanker. Amused, I showed my new title to Marta, but she had to read it three times before she saw the mistake. It's a perfect attribution, because we landscape architects who have no work and devise projects only for our own amusement are closer to wanking than landscaping. And *pajista*'s the perfect blend of artist and masturbator, I went on, already getting carried away. An artist of self-abuse, with no real vocation. Marta smiled and then she said, half-way between a statement and a question, but you don't masturbate, do you? Of course not, I said soothingly, except for when you refuse to make love to me four times a day.

A few hours after my presentation was when we went to eat at that cheap, glassed-in place just off the big boulevard. It was cold, and we decided to eat some kebab. I was waiting at the bar to pick up our order when the phone in my pocket vibrated, signaling the incoming text message. After reading it I looked over at Marta, and I could see from her expression that she'd sent me the text by mistake. I wasn't the intended recipient of that message or of the little heart it contained. She knew I hated messages with emoticons and text symbols, irritating substitutes for real emotion. Aware that her message had gone to the wrong address, Marta raised her eyes, saw me staring at her, and bit her lip. The man behind the counter delivered our food, an enormous pitcher of beer, and my cash receipt. I walked over to our table, carrying the tray. It trembled in my hands, as if I were the waiter on duty during an earthquake.

There's something ridiculous about breakups, because they oblige you to speak in set phrases no one's able to avoid. Like all the I love you's when love's at full tide, departing love has its catchphrases too.

There's no need to repeat them here. Marta broke up with me while we were eating kebab and I wanted to cry, but I concentrated on not getting grease stains on my clothes and not leaving traces of tzatziki in the corners of my mouth. Sometimes I used to joke with Marta or Carlos about the yogurt sauce that came with the kebabs we'd order when we were working at odd hours. There's still a little semen on your face, I'd say, when they'd failed to wipe the tzatziki off their mouths. Pivotal moments remain immortalized in your memory, associated with a circumstance, a detail, a place, a time of day. It was raining, you were wearing that sweater, a yellow car passed, a pigeon had been run over in the street. I didn't want my breakup with Marta to get spattered with yogurt sauce. I would always associate the end of our romance with that kebab lunch in Munich; no further details necessary.

Marta's message was addressed to her ex-boyfriend. They'd started seeing each other again a few months before, and their relationship had been reborn without my suspecting a thing. In Madrid, a week before our trip to Munich, his new CD on the racks in the Fnac store had attracted my attention for a second. I couldn't then guess that he'd soon be playing his music so thunderously in my life. I'd always been jealous of that guy, the man Marta had been with before I met her, just as I was jealous of her first love, a classmate of hers in ballet school. The only heterosexual male ballet dancer in all Madrid, and you get him as a classmate, I used to tell her, pretending to be indignant about my bad luck while she laughed at my foolishness. I wasn't the jealous type, given to suspicion, but a happy lover; I regretted the lost years before we met, when others were close to her and enjoying it and I was still unaware of her existence. Maybe such retroactive jealousy was absurd, but in fact Marta's sadness over breaking up with her singer boyfriend, the sadness she was immersed in when I met her, was the clearest declaration of her love for him. Now my retroactive jealousy was catching up with me, beating me in the race against time. Marta's past had returned, elbowing my future right off the track.

I was thinking about something to say to her, but she started to cry, and I didn't want everybody in the place looking at us. Stop it, calm down and eat, we'll talk later. But chewing turned out to be a ridiculously ordinary activity and no match for unleashed emotions. So we each left half of our kebab, still partly wrapped in silver foil, on our plates. Once we were out on the street, Marta continued to cry, but walking instead of facing each other made it easier for us to talk. I liked the Iranian director Abbas Kiarostami's movies, with those long conversations in cars, with shots of paths and highways seen through windows, because travel, which generally makes it very difficult to speak face-to-face and inclines you to keep your eyes on the road, is favorable to true confessions. My friend Carlos didn't like Iranian films; he made fun of them and pretended they formed a separate genre. Don't get all Persian movie on me, he'd joke. Marta would concede that the films were sometimes boring, but she understood my taste for them, for their slow, painstaking, even frozen tempo. I assured her more than once that agitation was only an attempt to fill the essential void.

I'd fooled around with the notion of becoming a film director. I would have loved to make Westerns about the days when the old West was coming to an end. When the railroad and the automobile arrived, and the solitary old gunfighters faded off into the twilight. However, I didn't have the strength of purpose required for such a calling. I was never interested in telling stories. I would have shot only isolated moments, moments with no narrative significance. So, condemned to be a maker of art films, one of the very people I found so ridiculous, I chose instead to calm my mother's and sisters' fears by getting a degree in architecture. However, I did shoot—without a camera—a film just for me. It was Marta's face in a luminous close-up that lasted almost five years and came to 3,784,320,000 (three billion seven hundred eighty-four million three hundred twenty thousand) frames, as I calculated by way of amusing myself when she wasn't there anymore.

I told Marta I thought she was basically trying to amend her past. You never accepted the fact of your separation, but if you think you can correct it now, you may be making a mistake. You can't change the past. But she kept shaking her head and repeating, really, it's not that, Beto, it's not that. I was so happy with you, you were so good for me. All of a sudden I saw myself as an emergency room doctor: he'd treated the patient's injuries, but now that she'd recovered, he couldn't do anything but discharge her and watch her walk away. I swear, the past was over for me, Beto, I'd overcome it. I nodded in assent, but I didn't agree. She kept talking. He's a new person now, and so am I. It followed, therefore, that the only one of us who'd turned into an old, broken person was me.

The strange thing was that some inner force, some proud, stubborn impulse, prevented me from stooping to recriminations. I had friends whose breakups were full of bitterness and reproach, and so I tried to achieve the only victory my situation allowed. Night fell, and Marta had yet to hear a complaint from me. Not even about the weeks when she'd been carrying on behind my back, about the time she'd dedicated to nurturing her new passion while starving and shutting down ours. I kept quiet about the wounds deception causes, because I could see the necessity of exploring the depths of the new love before taking definitive steps to seal up the well of the old. Actually, I wasn't fooling myself in those days, I was engaging in self-protection. I understand, I told her, you have to obey your heart, another set phrase that's indispensable when breaking up. I crossed the line into bitterness only when I declared I was unshakably convinced that she'd never stopped loving him throughout all our years together. You've never stopped loving him, I said.

We went to see that night's movie, for which we'd reserved tickets in the organization's office. Conferences always include showings of films, usually boring, pretentious stories with architecture or the world of art incorporated into the basic plot. The films that have the most to say about landscaping are the ones that don't emphasize it; you can hear better talk about it in an elevator or an office. The movie in question was a documentary about the postwar reconstruction of Munich and the recovery of its former splendor. It made me a little uneasy to hear one of the experts interviewed in the film recall the beautiful city and assert that the rise of nationalistic madness was a natural development. Conscious beauty always ends up provoking fascism, he claimed. The possession of beauty could turn you into a monster. Unable to concentrate on the film, I devoted my attention to Marta's lovely face and its special delicateness. I felt wounded at the thought that she was absorbed in the documentary. She was able to escape, to withdraw into something that wasn't us. Her concentration allowed me to scrutinize her skin and her features in the fluctuating light from the screen. When at some point she turned her gaze toward me and discovered that my eyes were fixed on her, she responded with a fairly counterfeit gesture of fatalism.

At the end of the film, Helga, who was surrounded by other conference volunteers, many of them retired people just interested in helping out, plus a couple of students curious about the proceedings and the presentations, invited us to have a drink with them in a nearby bar. The other Spanish landscaper will be there, Helga said encouragingly, trying to persuade us to go with them, but I told her we were tired. He told me he'd very much like to meet you, Helga insisted, and I noted an irony in her tone that seemed to be a response to the dismissive remark I'd made about Ripollés after my presentation. But when I gave Marta a questioning look, she shook her head, she didn't feel up to it, and I told Helga so. Besides, we have to be at the airport early tomorrow morning, I added. Yes, that's right, but I won't be able to drive you, one of my colleagues will, she said apologetically. What a shame. Well, get some sleep. Thanks for everything, I said, and tell Alex Gilipollez hello for me. I'll do that, she said. She gave us two affectionate kisses apiece and left, walking in her energetic, cheerful way, and Marta wanted to know why I'd said Alex Ripollés's name that way. That's how it's pronounced in German, I explained.

After we got back to the hotel room, I floated the possibility of making love as a tender farewell. I even offered my suggestion in comic terms. Let my body bid farewell to your body. Let my hands take leave of what they've caressed so long. My dick will say good--bye to your pussy and my hands to your ass. One last time, I'll kiss your lips and your skin with my lips. Think about them, our separation affects them too. But Marta refused: Please don't do this to me now, she said. She viewed my proposal as desperate sarcasm. In fact, when she got in bed she wouldn't let me see her naked, and her sudden modesty got me more excited than the supposed distance between us. So she was also denying my eyes the possibility of taking leave of her body, of that dear body that had been their favorite daily landscape and their primary source of joy in the past five years.

My wounded pride—hurt more by her refusal to give our last night together the real value of a last night, by her willingness to prevent our bodies from saying to each other the things they wanted to say, after so many years of mutual pleasure and goodwill—made me vain. It was vanity that led me to turn away, wrap myself in my own private duvet, and announce: I'm not going with you tomorrow. I'm not flying back home, I said, because I had neither home nor city nor country.

We slept fitfully, each of us awakened at times by the unsleeping presence of the other, so near but already on the way to being so far. I was inflamed with anger at myself for having failed to sense her state of mind, her renewed relationship. I thought I knew her, and yet there was so much I didn't know! I hadn't even been able to read in her eyes and her behavior the alarm she'd felt on meeting her old boy-friend again a few months before. Eventually I went back to sleep, and memories of the years we'd shared rolled through my mind, images evoked by nostalgia or spite. In the end, our separate duvets made it seem as though a knife had sliced the bed in half.

The next morning I listened to her showering and packing her bag in good time for the flight. Marta packed her bags the way she did everything in her life, with order and precision. For someone who planned things so carefully, our breakup must have been tor-ture. She shook me affectionately and I told her again, you go, I'm going to stay here for a few more days. She made several attempts to persuade me, even after the front desk called our room to inform us that the conference organization's car was waiting to take us to the airport. I didn't move. It was early, and I didn't feel like getting out of bed. My inertia could be understood as petty revenge. Let her return alone from the trip we'd set out on together. I think Marta couldn't cry anymore, so she made a weary gesture, like a defeated boxer, and bent down and brought her lips close to mine and kissed me good-bye. That was the last time we kissed each other on the lips. I pulled a pillow over my head, but I heard her leave. When the door closed and locked, there was an elec-tronic beep. I guessed it might be coming from the photocells, and this thought, this technological curiosity, struck me as ridiculous and inopportune and out of place.

At exactly twelve o'clock, a maid came to make up the room. The hotel reception had called me fifteen minutes earlier to advise me that checkout time was noon. I had told them I knew and then ignored the warning. The maid said she'd be back in ten minutes and closed the door politely.

In the shower, I found myself crying and aroused. Can you be hard and crushed at the same time? What do songs have to say about that? I stepped out of the shower and over to the bedside table to get my cell phone. Then I went back into the bathroom and sat on the closed toilet seat, scrolling through the collection of photos and short videos in the phone's memory. There they were, two or three shots of Marta naked at daybreak, part of a memorable visual tour of her body. There would be time to delete them later, but for now, they offered a substitute for what reality was denying me. I rose to my feet, yanking on my cock with my right hand while my left scrolled back and forth between those photographs of a happy Sunday now lost forever. I leaned against the glass door of the shower. The water was still beating down and getting hotter all the time. When I was reaching climax, enveloped in steam, the phone slipped out of my hand and fell onto the shower floor. I was slow to react, but then I rushed to recover my phone from the torrid water. Despite having scalded my hand, I hurriedly took the cell phone apart and dried its components with the hair dryer on its highest setting.

Out on the street, I found a supermarket, bought a kilo of rice, and put my cell phone in the bag with the rice. I'd heard one of my sisters recount how she'd used that method to save her phone after it fell into the toilet while she was answering messages. I was a sight to behold, walking down the street and holding up a bag of rice. The staff at the hotel offered to store my suitcase for me until I could find another, more affordable place to spend the night. The first lunches of the day were already being served in the breakfast room, and so in spite of my hunger, I went without breakfast.

Marta was the light of my life, the force that kept me going, that kept me fighting for projects when nobody wanted any. She was the embodiment of my good fortune, and with her at my side I felt invincible and lucky. I liked to joke about her name and tell her she'd come from Mars to rescue me so we could run away together. Marta, you come from Mars. Marta was my exile, my welcoming planet at a time when we felt vulnerable, expelled from our city, evicted from hearth and home. On stormy-weather days, when the economy was staining everything with winning and losing, Marta was my refuge and my shelter. But now I was outside the solar system, adrift without a compass, freezing with no heat to save me.

Are you all right? Are you crying? When I raised my head, I saw Helga bending over me, like someone peering down a well. I had my head buried in my hands and my elbows propped on my knees, and maybe I was crying or just trying to bear my humiliation. My feet were frozen and my nose red and running, from the cold, I thought, or perhaps from sadness. But you're like ice, is something wrong with you? Where's your girlfriend? A long gob of snot like a stalactite was stuck to my upturned face, and Helga handed me a tissue.

No, it's just that I'm on my own. To my surprise, Helga seemed to understand the ambiguity of my words. Words that were true, no matter what interpretation she gave them. Weren't you flying home today? Yes, but I decided to spend a few more days in Munich. Come on, get up, don't stay there. Why don't you come to the conference? Helga understood the situation without much explanation on my part or probing on hers; accumulated experience and intuitive knowledge enabled her to grasp what was left unsaid. The roundtable discussion starts in twenty minutes. Why don't you take part in it? Taking part seemed like a good idea. Taking part in anything at all.

And what may I ask is that? Helga pointed at the bag of rice, which I'd left on the bench when I stood up. I picked up the bag, thrust a hand into the grains, and fished out my cell phone. Helga smiled, but then she immediately looked at her watch. Hurry or we'll be late, she said, urging me on. As I walked along beside her, I tried to reactivate my phone. Nothing. Just the little black screen, reflecting my sad face, my disheveled hair, the collar of my overcoat. If you need to make a call, you can use my phone, Helga offered. No, thank you, I don't have anyone to call.

By the time they yielded the floor to me, after announcing my happy and unexpected inclusion in the roundtable, I'd been listening for a while as my colleagues, so young and so promising, discussed the answer to the first question, what's a landscape for? The confusion of languages so sterilized the conversation that it sounded like a discussion at the United Nations, despite the valiant efforts of three interpreters. Alex Ripollés raised his eyebrows when he saw me come in with Helga and join the group at the table. Besides him, the other participants were a young Bengali, so nervous that he never stopped moving, just as if he were sitting in a rocking chair; an intense Nigerian, wearing a loose-fitting *buba* shirt, *sokoto* trousers, and a *fila* hat; and lastly a shy, obese Korean. Alex had just presented his project, Chernobyl Park, which consisted in a re-creation of the day when the disaster at the Chernobyl Nuclear Power Plant occurred, set in a corner of Barcelona filled with characteristic features of that exact time. Apparently the day of the radioactive release coincided with the day of his birth in April 1986, and he explained that the intention of his project was to contrast life and death and the idea of time standing still. At the end of his talk, there was loud applause.

Secure in his indisputable attractiveness, Alex gave me an ironic look when I began to speak. I said: I don't know what a landscape's for. Because a landscape is a beautiful English garden, but also the border fence built to keep African migrants out of Melilla. I think it was Robin Lane Fox who asked an undergraduate at Oxford what the purpose of a garden was and got a wonderful answer: kissing, she said. Lives are spent in places, and our profession can't avoid the fact that those places are associated with every individual's personal experience. In the same park, your children take their first steps or your grandfather dies of a heart attack. Sometimes I try to put myself in Olmsted's place when he designed New York's Central Park, but the thing is, he was given the opportunity to transform a great metropolis, while we work at a different stage in the evolution of cities, we work on what's already done, we're on a rescue mission. I would like it if the places we landscape would encourage people to discover the world that's hidden to our eyes. Because we need to go back to looking at the real world instead of wandering around in a fiction or erecting a fantasy or choosing to escape. We need a mirror, a healing mirror, we need to fall in love with ourselves again, with the concrete, human fact of us, however imperfect that might be. I hadn't rehearsed or even thought about my talk, but defending the idea behind my park proposal with a general theory of landscape as archaic referent struck me as the right way to go about it, though the theory itself may have appeared obsolescent, given the technological brilliance and ingenuity of my fellow contestants. We can't allow—I went on—architecture and urbanism to be entertaining for those who practice them but impossible to appreciate for those who have to endure them. Modernity, true modernity, consists in finding ourselves again and in rediscovering houses, streets, time, dawn, twilight, the sun, clouds; in rediscovering the organic. Maybe I was starting to sound ridiculous, but the interruptions while I waited for Helga to translate what I'd said into German helped keep my strength up. I continued: I always remember something I heard Buñuel say. He was an atheist, he said, he didn't believe in God, except for the god invented by men, the lie they put in place to comfort themselves with. But if the alternative was science and technology as high-precision solutions for everything, he preferred, by far, the slapdash idea of God.

After I finished, Alex Ripollés joked about my little speech. Sometimes it seemed more like a religion lesson—would you really rather have God than a good cell phone? Everything you said sounded to me like a treatise on gardening as self-help. When Helga translated his words, the audience laughed. I don't agree with you at all, he continued, but I really love the project you presented in the competition, those sand clocks, the idea of sitting and watching time pass. Nevertheless, he went on, our job isn't to console the citizenry, public spaces aren't rehabilitation wards; our job is to shake people up, bounce them around, upbraid them. Not calm them down, never that, just the opposite. We have to challenge and upset people, strike them, make them uncomfortable. Helga's translation was virtually simultaneous with Alex's speech.

Oh, really?—I interrupted him—Is that what you like? That's our task? Let's give it a try. Let me try it with you, I said, and I got up from my seat and started yanking him by the lapels, shaking him, bouncing him around on his rolling chair. This is what you think we ought to do with people, right? What I'm doing to you now. If I see a cruel film where the characters are humiliated and mistreated, you know what I always want to do? Apply that same treatment to the director and the screenwriter. Helga was late in translating my words, but the audience was no longer paying any attention to what she was saying, they were focused on my inappropriate but so far bloodless violence. She laughed, amid the general discomfort. Alex Ripollés offered no resistance, but behind his neat façade of relaxed superiority, he was tense. Had Marta been there, I wouldn't have exploded, and solitude's always conducive to self-pity and tears, but that auditorium was practically an invitation to fury.

So I vented all my distilled rage on Alex Ripollés at the roundtable, which despite its name included no table and nothing round, except for the young Korean designer, whose tone of voice was identical to that of a six-year-old child. At the peak of my angry fit, I unfortunately gave Alex's wheeled chair a hard push. The discussion was taking place on a platform raised some six inches above the level of the few people in attendance. My push sent the chair rolling across the platform, over the edge, and into the shallow abyss. Alex Ripollés pitched face-first onto the floor, followed an instant later by the chair, which struck him from behind. The room became as silent as a funeral home. Some members of the audience and two of the speakers helped to set the fallen man on his feet. Alex Ripollés calmed everybody down. I'm all right, he said. Somebody retrieved the empty chair and put it back in its place on the platform. The panel's moderator harshly condemned my attitude, his German words thudding like rocks at a stoning. I'd better stop translating, Helga said to me, and you'd better go. I'm sorry, I said, I want to apologize, I was just trying to demonstrate my point of view. But I decided to leave it there, because I was getting looks of enormous contempt, mixed with a bit of fear, from everyone around me.

I stepped wretchedly out of the auditorium, left the redbrick heart of the convention center, and looked for the street with the most traffic. Meanwhile

I tried to turn on my cell phone, but nothing inside it responded to my desperation. I walked along the big commercial street and came upon a nearby cinema, the Kino Rio, which featured two screens. Next to the movie house was a fruit stand, and behind that a telephone store. I went in and waited until the young employee, busy with another customer, could help me. All the advertisements surrounding the cell phone display showed young, beautiful men and women in the blissful world of permanent connection. When the kid was free, I handed him my phone and managed to make him understand I'd had a domestic accident, an accident in the shower, omitting the masturbation part. He shook his head, took out the battery, and confessed there was nothing he could do. So then, in a gesture of survival, I chose the fanciest phone in the place. I want this one, I declared. *Eine gute Wahl,* he said. Good choice.

With the renewed vigor that only the acquisition of consumer goods can inject, I went back to the convention center. I had to apologize; I had to beg everyone's pardon. When I entered, the discussion was just coming to a close. Someone had removed my empty chair. I sat down in the back of the auditorium, in the last row. I took my new phone out of its box and inserted the SIM card from my old phone. My bank account had reached zero, but it was urgent for me to start regaining my place in the world. The phone's battery was nearly dead, so I had to find an electrical outlet to plug into. I looked around, but then the session ended. I waited until I saw Alex Ripollés moving toward the door and went to meet him, holding out my hand. I'm sorry, I said. But he didn't even look at me, he merely hissed go fuck yourself.

The conference director approached, said something in German I didn't understand, and moved on. Helga, who'd been observing us, walked over to me. With a gesture, I indicated my failure to comprehend the man's words. He just said something about your behavior, she explained. Something like, the way you act puts you in the wrong. *Die Manieren, deren du dich bedient hat, setzen dich ins Unrecht. Die Manieren* are your manners, the way you behave. *Recht haben* means to be in the right, *setzen* is to put. So we could translate *ins Unrecht setzen* as to put in the wrong. A bit complicated, to tell the truth.

Helga's detailed explanation had a good effect on me. Turning the moment into a German lesson diminished the seriousness of my conduct. She stayed right where she was and asked, you sure you're all right? I nodded my head and—I think—apologized again. Your lunch vouchers have probably expired. Will you let me take you someplace nice for dinner? My treat. No, no, I said, trying to refuse. The last thing I needed just then was the pity of strangers. Come on, you can't hang around here all by yourself.

Outside it was dark, and Helga armed herself against the cold with an overcoat. We walked down the avenue, getting farther and farther away from the convention center. If you like sauerkraut, I know where they make the best in the city. I consented to her proposal without much enthusiasm. For the first time, I noticed that Helga was tall and slender, and that though she was past sixty her face retained a childlike expression. She had wrinkles around her eyes and above her upper lip, but she gave her smiles an ironic twist, which combined with her poise to radiate self-confidence. Her hair was the color of ashes and worn simply, pulled back from her broad forehead and gathered in a long ponytail. She had very thin eyebrows and a strong nose, the crowning touch on a countenance that openly declared her personality. It occurred to me that she must have been really good-looking when she was young, and the thought sounded insulting. Good-looking when young is an unlucky expression, a professor at the university once told me, correcting something I'd said in the course of an informal conversation. What you are when you're young is young; beauty travels in a different lane. Or it ought to travel in a different lane, he specified. I nearly slipped on some ice, but Helga deftly caught me by the arm. Be careful, the sidewalks freeze over at this time of night.

I appreciated the warmth of the packed restaurant and the beer we drank at the bar while a waiter who'd conspired with Helga sought out an opening for us at one of the long wooden tables. We sat down, surrounded by noisy Bavarians. I fixed my attention on the foreign conversations—sometimes more on the waggling mustaches than on the words themselves—and the magnificent tone of their cordial but heated arguments. I was also interested in avoiding an uncomfortable conversation with Helga, who ordered our food but hardly touched it, while I scarfed down a variety of sausages, unable to suppress the childish thought that they were penises and even straining to imagine the faces of their owners at the moment when they parted company. Sometimes, when everyone laughed, she translated the joke for me, and she explained to someone who wanted to know that I was Spanish. And by the way, where in Spain are you from? From Madrid, I said. Ah, I love Madrid, what a city. The last time I went there was a while ago, but I really enjoyed walking in the area around the Opera and the Royal Palace. I like opera a lot, she said. She told me she'd joined a choral society three years before, and after having spent her whole life convinced that she sang horribly, she was proud that the director had praised her. I had a complex about singing my whole life, she told me with a smile, and in the end it turns out I could sing well all along. Oh, yes? And what do you sing? I asked. Once we went to Madrid to sing Schubert. And without a blush, using a clear undertone, she launched into what might have been a Lied by Schubert, had I been able to identify it. Then she began to speak normally again. There's always a mime at one side of the Royal Opera in Madrid, she told me. He's very amusing, he makes fun of people as they pass. She was surprised to see my horrified expression. I explained that I hated mimes. Don't ask me why, but they upset me, they get on my nerves; that mixture of tragic clown and prancing referee brings out my aggression. And when they do that thing with the glass wall...

I stopped and imitated a mime's glass wall routine. She laughed. You do that very well. Yes, I could earn my living as a Spanish mime in Germany. Besides, that way I wouldn't have problems with the language. Since it's clear they don't want unemployed Spaniards around here, they just want engineers. Good, so you're an architect. Yes, the truth is, for landscape architects in Spain right now, one professional option is to become a street mime, it's the area where we're getting most of our jobs. Helga responded to my joking tone. Of course, the mime creates invisible works of architecture. Exactly, just like me, I assured her. Everything I create is invisible, it never gets done. She laughed good-heartedly. You should be an actor, she added, obscurely praising me. Marta was an actress, I said.

Once Marta's name was spoken, I visibly clouded over as memories rained down on me. Helga asked me some questions about our relationship and our unexpected breakup, and I gave her some rather shameless answers. It wasn't hard to let myself go a little and tell her about our last hours in Munich; after all, until that moment I hadn't been able to share my story with anyone. Hiding my sadness was the complicated part. Two or three probing queries from Helga about our mutual past, Marta's and mine, were enough to set me off, and I segued into an interminable monologue that went all the way back to the beginning of our relationship, to Marta's sadness at having been left by her Uruguayan singer boyfriend and my efforts to help her recover her happiness, to our working together, our living together, the good days, the bad days. She was obsessed with her age, which was twenty-seven, I said; she'd been gloomy ever since her birthday, convinced that her life was slipping through her fingers, and she freely admitted her distress. I get the impression that our breakup and her reunion with her old boyfriend have more to do with that, with a personal crisis, than with some aspect of our relationship.

Oh, come on, said Helga, who by that point had drunk a goodly amount of white wine. I can't believe anyone has a crisis at the age of twenty-seven. In that case, what are women who reach fifty-seven supposed to do? Organize a mass suicide? And I'm sixty-three, so how about me? She made me laugh and went on talking about women and the passage of time and the difficulties of living as a couple and then she said, all this sorrow you're feeling now will help you grow. I don't want to grow any more, I said, I'm tall enough, but she ignored my joke. It might have been the fault of my limitations in speaking English. It relaxed me to have to express myself in such a rudimentary way, in a language foreign to me. It will make you better, Helga was going on. Sorrow is an investment. I shook my head dejectedly, unable to identify the banking system that would let me speculate with all the sorrow deposited inside me.

Aware of the difficulties involved in extracting me from my self-absorption, Helga talked about practical matters. Where was my luggage, did I have a hotel for the night, had I asked the airline to change my ticket, when did I plan to go back to Spain. The best thing for you right now is to be with your friends, your family, the people who love you. But I had thought that was a club Marta was the president of. Helga and I were gradually getting drunk, and I was talking to her about my family and my siblings, all girls and all quite a bit older than me, because I was a late baby, a boy who unexpectedly arrived ten years after the youngest of the four girls. They could be of little help to me in a situation like this. I told Helga I intended to find a cheap hotel and spend a few more days in Munich before returning to Madrid, where I would have to deal with the separation, moving out, finding another apartment. I said I didn't have a return ticket, and the first thing I thought of was the cost of my own spite, my stupid purchase of the most expensive cell phone I could find. When the bill arrived, Helga insisted on paying it. I invited you as my guest, she said. But let me ask you a question that's got me curious. That text message you told me about—do you really think Marta sent it to you by mistake? The question surprised me. I mean, the most normal explanation is that she made a real error, but all the same, that error saved her from doing a lot of explaining, from telling you everything. The message was a strategy. Don't you think? Don't you think she sent it to you not by mistake but on purpose, as a way of informing you about what was going on?

I confessed I hadn't thought about that. I had no response to her question. It wasn't as though I'd ever seen Marta struggling to tell me the latest news about her feelings. Let's do this: I don't live far from here, you can spend the night at my house, and then tomorrow you can pick up your luggage and we can try to make arrangements for your return ticket through the conference organization. Maybe they'll pay for a new one or at least find you a cheap flight—they have promotional agreements with various airlines. I thanked her, but I refused everything for five minutes. In the street, I continued to turn down all her proposals, but I followed her to the taxi stand and we climbed into the first available cab.

Entering her home obliged me to exercise caution, despite my alcoholic euphoria. Was there something going on between us that I wasn't processing? Helga looked quite comfortable, but the idea that she was seducing me struck me as grotesque. She was just being friendly. A woman like her had to feel some concern after finding a Spaniard weeping on a bench in the street and then watching him, in the course of a roundtable discussion, push a fellow landscape architect off the stage. From all appearances, she was a spritely retiree who worked as a volunteer at the landscaping conference, and her reaction was rather a friendly offer of hospitality than inappropriate flirtatiousness. An enormous poster for F. W. Murnau's film *The Last Laugh* was on one wall of her living room, while two abstract paintings, lost in shadow, were on another.

She invited me to take a seat. Do you live alone? I asked. No, no, she said, pointing to a totally gray cat, which was at that moment rubbing against her shoes. She took it in her arms and stroked it between the eyes. The cat kept staring at me the whole time, with a look that was more than human; it was smart. Helga told me the cat's name was Fassbinder. She asked if I'd have something to drink, and in the end we both opted for vodka. She'd just received a bottle of Polish vodka as a gift from the girl who cleaned house for her, and she hardly ever drank and didn't often have guests. After we toasted each other, she explained that she'd lived alone for more than fifteen years, ever since she and her husband separated. I've been in the situation you're in now, she said. I made an effort to appreciate what a tragedy the separation must have been for her, an older woman abandoned by the husband she'd spent her life married to, but sentimentality is ego-centric, it's a nationalism of the self, it always makes you more of a victim, more wronged, more import-ant than anyone else.

They had two children. The older one was Volker, nearly forty, and his little sister, Hannah, was two years younger. Your husband left you for a younger woman, of course. No, no, they worked together, they were the same age. Well, she's more or less my age, and my husband's four years older than I am. Their love story was an arduous affair—it took them years to acknowledge and admit it. That was a very sad moment for me, most of all because I was going to be left on my own. She held up the vodka bottle again and shook it, and I saw the blade of bison grass—also solitary—on the bottom. But we get along well, and he always lets me use his house in Mallorca over the Christmas holidays. It used to be our house, we bought it when we were married; it's on a gorgeous cove. When we divided up the property, he got the house in Mallorca and I got this apartment. But I still spend the end of every year down there. Your children go with you? No, no, they've always got other plans for Christmas and New Year's. They like Mallorca only in the summer, with the sun and the beach. At the end of the year, they go where the snow is. I pre-fer the beach in winter. Me too, I said, but actually it was Marta who preferred beaches in winter, she'd rather walk on the sand pulling down her sweater sleeves than stroll along in a bathing suit. I've got five grandchildren, how about that? I'd lost the thread of the conversation, but I whistled when I heard about the five grandchildren, and the cat, which was lying on the carpet, twisted its neck around and gave me an annoyed look. Do you and Marta have any children?

The question surprised me. Children? There was definitely a time when Marta and I would have had children, when our finances were in better shape and our work more lucrative. I wanted children, but she was a little younger than me, I told Helga, going into detail for no apparent reason. I went on, in my tentative English: when I told Marta that the world needed her to have children as a way of improving the human landscape, she laughed at me and said that was a very childish and romantic idea. Children can't have children, Marta used to say, just to provoke me. Helga laughed. Love's always childish, isn't it? So what? The first person who cut a flower and gave it to someone behaved like a stupid romantic, I'm sure. But being a stupid romantic takes a lot of courage. Although I was looking at Helga, I opened my eyes even wider, surprised by the firmness of the judgment she'd just pronounced. I opened my eyes, even though they were already open. I observed her with growing interest instead of looking through her, which was what I'd been doing since we met. I remember my husband said something really corny on our first date, but I found it charming: *Deine Augen sind wie die Karibik.*

It means something like, your eyes are the color of the Caribbean Sea. I had to agree with Helga's husband, so many years after that first date, because her eyes were still shining, still a transparent turquoise. I burst out laughing when he said it, but in the end I preferred that corny moment to the many years that came afterward, Helga assured me. The years when the febrility that seemed so ridiculous at the time was gone. Febrility, does that word exist in English? she asked. Helga was often slightly hesitant about pronouncing English words. Of course it exists, I told her, and if it doesn't, we'll invent it.

It would be complicated to relate our subsequent conversation. We jumped from topic to topic. I explained the animosity I felt toward Alex Ripollés, how it had accumulated over the course of several competitions; she talked about her first post-separation attack of rage, when she tore up all the photographs her husband appeared in and then spent months trying to recover them from old rolls of film or her children's photo albums. It's idiotic to attack your memories, she said, it's as stupid as it would be to trample on your hand because one day it caressed your lost love. I assented to this observation without much conviction. Everything turns out bad, she declared, that's a condition inherent in the fact of being alive. She spoke as if remembering the exact words of some book.

Helga was amused, and when she smiled, her tense jaw muscles relaxed. She made a little fun of my state of mind and then said, deep down, I miss feeling as wounded as you do now. She told me that when she found me in the park, sitting by myself on a bench, she'd thought about her father. My father was Russian, he came to Germany before the war, even though he didn't know anyone here. His hands were like yours. He was always more Russian than German. My mother sort of trained him, she Germanized him. Helga raised her glass of vodka and clinked it against mine in a toast. *Na zdorovie!* I said, suddenly aware that I had a companion there in the desert.

I ought to stay and live in Germany too, I remarked, after she finished telling me about her father's decision to immigrate. Don't even think about it, she said, you Spaniards get all faded here, like plants without sun. Although this country's very well organized, it's not so free. Sometimes I feel like I'm living inside a giant clockwork mechanism, but Spaniards—you all float in the air. That has its problems, but it's more, I don't know, what's the word, more euphoric. The Spaniard's tragedy is that he can't be happy in any other country in the world, she said. Spanish is his element. I know some people from Mallorca who've come here to work, but my father was different, he stayed here for my mother. Because my parents' love was truly amazing—the way they loved each other made a permanent impression on me. I aspired to be part of a couple like my parents. It was almost a recurring daydream, a steady desire. And although I wasn't happy with my husband, I thought it was essential for us to stay together, I clung to the image of my parents, which was what I wanted to emulate. The image of my father, playing old Russian songs for my mother on the record player in the living room...Helga subsided into silent remembering. I knew without her telling me that she'd got her eyes from her mother, I was sure of it. And so on the day when my husband decided to leave me, after a long period of deceit and mutual lies, my biggest disappointment was the thought that I hadn't been capable of living as my parents had, of maintaining a loving relationship like theirs. My ideal world collapsed, but I was lying to myself, no doubt about it. The way you're lying to yourself now. Because people don't wound us; what wounds us is seeing our ideals destroyed, that's what's so shattering.

And after it was over, you never got together with anyone else? My question hung in the air for a few seconds. It's complicated, she said, men look to women for sex, but they don't want our company, our conversation, they don't want to really share things, they just don't want that. Right, I said, unable to come up with a valid argument to absolve the half of humanity whose defense attorney, at that moment, I was. Sure, Helga said, I had some typical office affairs. I got involved with somebody, one of his friends, but mostly with the idea of pissing off Götz. Götz was my husband. I laughed. Pissing off Götz, what a great title for a movie. Then it occurred to me that soon I too would always talk about Marta in the past tense. Marta was, Marta did, Marta said. Yes, Helga said consolingly, but don't worry about that, you'll speak in the past tense about almost everything. She pointed at a black-and-white photograph on a bookshelf, a picture of a beautiful young woman sitting on the ground with her knees tucked under her chin. Was that your mother? I asked. No, it was me. I noticed the rare expression of past and present in a single sentence: it was me. The aura of that youthful beauty settled over her in a thick, nostalgic silence, that and the light of a lamp standing way off in a corner made her look attractive, and I pressed my lips against her lips in a light kiss. She didn't reject it, but when I grasped the back of her head and tried to pull her toward me, she stopped me with some force, covering my mouth with one hand and pushing me away. No, no, don't do that. Can you imagine how ridiculous? Please, no, I'm not out for romance, really, you've got me wrong. I've said good-bye to all that. I hauled you up here to keep you from lying down in the gutter, not to seduce you. She crumpled a smile at me, the way you crumple an empty pack of cigarettes. Let's talk, tell me about your work, your projects.

I felt ridiculous and uncomfortable. I shook my head and produced a grin. Then I tried for a while to explain what had brought me to my profession, why

I had studied it, what about it appealed to me, until I succeeded in boring myself. I think we should go to bed, she said. We've had too much to drink, and it seems to me your judgment's a bit cloudy. There are enough issues in your life that need settling without adding me to that muddle you've got in there, she said, touching my forehead with a fingertip. She sounded to me like a mother giving advice, but with an almost hurtful note of irony, and in a German accent that lent authority to everything she said in English. At a certain point, her detached manner made me suspect she was making fun of me. Tomorrow she'd laugh about it with her girlfriends. So I take a young man home and he jumps on me and starts kissing me, incredible, don't you think, Greta? These young people today, what can they be thinking, these Spaniards are a cheeky bunch. They're nothing but Africans, offering sex to German tourists of a certain age, like what happened to Inge in Kenya.

All of a sudden I felt violent, and then ashamed. I followed her to the guest quarters, formerly her son's room. She pointed out the bathroom, and when I had finished discharging a copious and torrential flood of urine, she was standing outside the door with two folded towels. It pained me again to see her planted there, surely longer than she'd counted on, waiting for the river of piss accumulated in my bladder to run dry. She was wearing a dress that offered a glimpse of her admirable breasts and of the brassiere that presented them like desserts on a tray, and the fine purplish vein visible on one pale mound excited me so much that I kissed her again, but this time I didn't let her control the distance between us. I drew the towels out of her hands. She put her arms around my waist and pulled me close, so that our bodies made contact. I had on a short-sleeved shirt, and she thrust a hand under one sleeve and up to my shoulder in a caress her fingernails turned into gentle scratching. I stepped backward, half carrying her to the foot of my bed, sat her down, and undressed in front of her, hurriedly, in four spasmodic movements, without touching her except to push her hair off her face.

Naked before her—I on my feet and she seated on the bed—I offered myself to her desire; I wanted to be a sort of unwrapped gift. Helga interpreted my position as an indication that I expected her to suck my cock, and her subtle movement made it clear she wasn't going to do that. She grabbed my hand and yanked me onto the mattress. Then she rolled over on top of me, or rather beside me. She started taking off her clothes, struggling awkwardly. My assistance served only to complicate things, but soon the laborious process became amusing and even exciting.

Although from time to time she laid her hand on my cock, which was growing unreservedly, Helga displayed an almost adolescent shyness. After I succeeded in tugging her dress all the way down, I came up against her panties, the underwear of someone who hadn't conscientiously prepared herself for such an exercise in disrobing. But the uneasiness caused by the inducements of a body with evident imperfections vanished when she herself removed her bra, whose hooks my fingers had fumbled with clumsily and in vain. Two breasts emerged, white and unbound, swaying like fruit on a tree. Now, for the first time, Helga showed a trace of forcefulness and even pride, rubbing her chest against mine, confident in her desirability, less reticent than she'd been until that moment.

We kissed messily, our kisses growing wetter with each onslaught. Her tongue was sour from the vodka and mine furry with drunkenness. She tousled my curly hair. I believe she'd told me at dinner she liked my curls, but neither she nor I had thought she'd end the night playing with them, tangling her fingers in them while I stretched out full length, replacing the cat as the object of her caresses. Helga's pussy wasn't easy to reach, because she shoved my hand away several times, not at all coyly. It became imperative for me to stimulate her, practically speaking, but mostly because every time her fingers grazed my member, I felt an uncontainable surge. I wanted her to come before I did to settle any dispute about priorities. With Marta, that was almost always the way things went. I'd manage to make her come without taking my eyes off her face, which tensed with a hint of annoyance as she lost her self-control but none of her beauty. From that point on, I could let myself be manipulated or dominated, and I could finally let myself come. Helga guessed my mental process, it seemed, because she put her hand on her sex and tried to arouse herself.

The scene was complicated, the bed was small. The bedspread slipped off of it before we made any decision about getting between the sheets. When I put my hands on her ass to help her climb on top of me, I noticed that the liberated flesh of her hips was shaking too. I clutched it tight. But far from tempering my excitement or sending me irretrievably into nostalgia for Marta's lost ass, as perfect and smooth as an apple, the feel of Helga's flesh only increased the delirium of carnality I was plunging into.

It was Helga who tore off the covers and dived hastily between the sheets, with the shyness that can return with age, just as senility can entail a childish lack of inhibitions. She smiled at me, naked and alone on the other side of the bedclothes, completely exposed while she was covered to the chin. I jumped comically into the sheets and we were skin-to-skin again, but now with the doubled stimulation of being under cover, where everything happens out of sight. I got on top of her, but when I began prospecting for penetration, I encountered a firm opposition I was unable to overcome. I tried my agile fingers again, aware now that it would require some work to make her wet through the buffer of her pubic hair. I'd grown used to Marta's shaved sex, and to how simple it had been to spot the moisture glistening on her thighs.

Helga stopped my hand with hers and shifted around a little. No, she said, the problem is it's been too long since the last time I did this. It was a curt statement, nothing at all like a request. She closed her eyes and let her head fall backward onto the pillow. I moved my cock closer to her sex, but with no intention of penetrating her—I just rubbed myself against her there for a minute or two. And this shuts down if you let a long time pass without using it? I tried to make that sound more like a real question than an ironic remark, but Helga responded with a guffaw. Yes indeed, she said, it seals itself hermetically. I remembered the shelf in the bathroom, got out of bed quickly, and ran over to it. With the speed of a thief, I sought out a jar of moisturizing cream I thought I'd seen in there. None of the brands was familiar, and all the labels were in German, but I found the hand lotion and dashed back with it into the bedroom. This will help, I said. I knelt on the bed in front of her and rubbed some cream onto my cock. That amused her, and she put some of the white stuff on her fingertips and began to rub it in resolutely and skillfully. Her hand slid up and down my penis so vigorously and excited me so much that I pulled the covers away from her breasts and climaxed on them in a torrent. She didn't stop stroking and then squeezing me, with the dedication one applies to emptying a ketchup bottle. My semen ran over her breasts and down to her armpits in long streaks.

I dropped on top of her, overcome by my arduous return to gravity and normal consciousness. I noticed our shared wetness and the lotion on both of us, and I recognized her ironic grin, just above the bedclothes, which she'd once again pulled up to her throat. We remained unmoving while the sticky substances between us solidified. She stroked the nape of my neck with her fingertips and scratched my scalp through my hair and I wondered how the fuck I'd wound up in that particular location and what the fuck I could do to escape. Unreason was now being replaced by rationality, always so inconvenient.

She rocked her body to open a space between us, and then she said, wait, and resettled herself. I'd probably been crushing her, and so I moved away until I was stopped by the edge of the bed, while she tacitly maintained her position, like a soldier who falls back to his trench after a battle and concentrates his efforts on holding the line. We both stared at the ceiling, looking for an escape, and her sigh sounded a little embarrassed. Well, now comes the hard part, right? she joked. No, I said, but I couldn't come up with anything to add to that.

I'd better go away and let you sleep, she suggested after I started breathing noisily, half out of drunkenness and half out of weariness. I hardly slept at all last night, I said to justify myself. Marta was so near but at the same time so far. And now, one night later, so far but so near. I'd keeled over in the bed, suspending my active life, but now I held Helga back when she tried to get up. No, stay, I said. Although she appreciated the thought, she shook her head. I'm sorry, she said, excusing herself, I'm way out of practice, I feel a little absurd. I didn't say anything, and silence overtook her explanations. I was still holding her around the hips, with her bulging belly under my arm. You know, I haven't been with a man in almost twelve years, she confessed. Cut the crap, I said. I immediately regretted saying that, because it sounded like a taunt. I wanted her to look at me, but she wouldn't raise her eyes. So many years without sexual relations had made the moment almost a second loss of virginity for her. In spite of intoxication and exhaustion, I tried my hardest to convey tenderness. At least the tenderness she deserved.

I stroked her loose thighs. Despite the tolerable perfume she was wearing, the smell of her nearness suddenly seemed muddy. When I touched my semen while caressing her, it felt disagreeably cold. Our sexual presence was totally uncomfortable and dirty. I tried talking, and we were able to keep up a short conversation. She apologized and said she'd surely caught me at a weak moment. I denied it. When you and Marta were together, did you sleep with other women sometimes? she asked me. I rocked my head back and forth. Only three in five years, I answered truthfully. An old girlfriend, someone quite a lot wilder than Marta in bed, had captured me after a party and given me a short, intense update session on what I'd been missing. When I finally got away, it was with a bad conscience. But not as bad as the second time, one summer when Marta spent a couple of weeks at the beach with her parents and I wound up with a girl I'd met through friends, a girl from Logroño: we went to bed in her hotel room, I came, and then I absconded, I barely said good-bye. The rudeness of the falsely virtuous. The third woman was the most recent; after sexual activity with Marta had been reduced to such a degree that fucking became a physiological necessity, the roulette wheel stopped on a photographer friend of ours, a woman of Guinean origin who helped put together our catalog and came to the office to take pictures of our best 3-D models. After we got to know each other better, the photographer and I, we had three or four encounters characterized by perspiration and aerobic passion, but with no hope for the future and with not the smallest emotional connection between us. She knew Marta, and she'd tell me, you've got such a pretty girlfriend, she's ravishing. She'd photographed Marta on several occasions during her stint as a promising actress, and she talked about her, about the woman I lived with, as if we were chatting over some beers in a bar instead of frolicking naked on the bed in her apartment.

I didn't recount those details to Helga. But she laughed at the way I told her about the three outside women in five years, almost in the style of a mathematical equation. Then I said I supposed those workplace accidents on the relationship-building site were signs of how things between Marta and me were already getting bogged down, slowly, even before her old boyfriend the Uruguayan singer returned like a deferred dream. The eighth time I referred to him as the Uruguayan singer, Helga teased me. You say Uruguayan singer as if you were talking about some exotic bird species. Well, maybe that's what he is, I answered evasively. Sex is almost always the most reliable gauge of a relationship, Helga opined, making a conversational detour. My husband stopped insisting we make love. He had a way all his own, forthright and abrupt, he'd get in bed and pressure me into doing it, but then he stopped. He cheated on me with his lover for seven years before we separated. Seven years? And you didn't notice? Yes, I mean, I don't know, I thought he was letting off steam, so to speak, I even found it somewhat convenient, but I never imagined he could get into another serious relationship. Now I understand I was mistaken, but at least I've stopped feeling guilty about it. That was the worst, abandoned *and* guilty. I feel guilty too, I said.

All at once the idea of a long and stable relationship, the shadowy realm of marriage, repelled me. I'd spent the evening feeling sorry for myself because

Marta canceled the promised happiness of growing old together, and now something told me that even had I gone down that lengthy road, it would have led inevitably to catastrophe. It was better for love to break apart in its splendor, and too risky to subject it to the passage of time. Oh no, what stupidity. Who knows the truth? Who cares about the truth, the truth that will come to pass whether you want it to or not, if just walking toward it slowly is beautiful?

Helga had big nipples, and the intense pink of her areolae contrasted with her moon-colored flesh. I glimpsed them every time she shifted her folded forearms, coyly careful about rearranging her breasts before she went on talking to me. The couple is the only remedy we have against loneliness, she said, but we all know it's not perfect. Then she added something in German: *Einsamkeit.* Loneliness, she explained. German's pretty, I said, I've always wanted to learn it.

She smiled and rolled onto her side. One summer in Mallorca, back in the days when my husband and I still spent our summers there together, I gave German lessons to the son of some Spanish friends. I thought she was implying she'd gone to bed with him, but she was shocked when she heard me taking that for granted. Don't you know any German? No, none at all. She touched my nose and said *Nase.* Then she brushed my lips and said *Lippen.* Then my eyes, *Augen.* My hair, *Haar.* And my ear, *Ohr.* And when she touched my chin and said *Kinn,* I put my hand on her breast. *Brust.* I thought she meant I was being brusque, abrupt. Or that she was talking to me like those masters who command their dogs in German because they obey more readily. But that wasn't it. We smiled at each other, and she reached for my cock and named it in German, *der Penis,* but couldn't avoid blushing. Surely not, I said, no one uses the scientific name, do they? We say *la polla* in Spanish. *La polla?* Yes. *Der Schwanz.* Her hands were still oily from the lotion, and her lesson in linguistic anatomy had succeeded in arousing me again. I thrust my forearm between her legs and lifted her forcefully. Then I applied myself to exciting her, looking for creases and bone ends, all the while studying her mouth and forehead for her reactions. Something in her exploded at once, the result of overstimulation and the accumulated energy of desire, repressed for so many years and now bursting out like water through a broken dam. Helga clutched the sheets in her fists and let herself go, groaning and even screaming so loudly that I put my hand over her mouth a couple of times. I was worried about what her German neighbors would think, accustomed as they were to silence from the solitary divorcée on the third floor. My conscientious work paid off when I was able to watch her come, so hard, so movingly.

Then, having felt my erection, she lowered her head to suck my cock, but not before saying, I'm ter-

rible at this. But I didn't let her go beyond an enthusi-
astic and generous demonstration before flinging her
onto the mattress, and this time I indeed penetrated
her. We reached a point where she couldn't attain any
more pleasure than she'd already felt and I couldn't
reach my goal. We fell into a sort of mechanical process whose result was more strenuous exercise than
wild passion. A blockage of the senses, which were
somewhat numb and refused more ecstasy. And so I
pulled my over-moistened penis out of her and jerked
myself off, this time coming on her navel and the
folds of her white belly.

There was something in my action that had to
do with erotic fury and defiance. Not toward Helga,
needless to say, but toward the sense of unhappi-
ness and abandonment the memory of Marta gave
me. Helga made no move to caress or kiss me, but
instead she pulled me down onto her calm body and
embraced me, and then she let me roll off of her, turn
my back, and flee into sleep, without subjecting me
to any aggravating, sentimental stroking of my hair
and shoulders. If she felt suddenly abandoned, as she
evidently was, she hid it discreetly. When I awoke
after a first leaden snooze, charged with sexual satis-
faction and alcohol, she pretended to be asleep at my
side, even though her breathing gave her away.

Later in the night, she started snoring, a series of
little snorts, and I felt a bit disgusted and ridiculous.
I moved farther away to my side of the bed, which

seemed pretty narrow now that we weren't sharing our bodies. I tried to go back to sleep, downcast, depressed, and shattered, empty except for Marta in my memory, including the memory I carried in my skin. In the course of our evening, Helga had told me the trauma of being left always leads you to idealize the person who's gone; you carefully make him or her into someone more perfect, more human, more desirable, more irreplaceable. We do it, she told me, to cause ourselves more harm. That ideal we've constructed oppresses us; it's a way of insulting ourselves that for months and years disables us from loving anyone more than we love it, and it makes us look upon men and women as pitiful pastiches of the unparalleled creature we've just lost. Then one day we find that our memory becomes more precise and more accurate, and from that moment we can resume thinking about being less unhappy. Helga had told me all this as she lay on the sofa, and the conviction she said it with seduced me.

That night I didn't have the strength to go over more details of my conversation with Helga or reflect on the friendliness and naturalness of her manner. I forgot the delicacy she'd shown toward me. The sexual culmination of our meeting had blurred the traces of the touching care she'd lavished on me from the moment she found me sitting on a street bench, broken and wretched. Helga's every word, her every gesture had been a comfort to me, a solace I would take too long to appreciate. She wasn't just a maternal refuge for the solitary, forsaken human waste Marta's departure had turned me into. No. There was more. It was the intelligence, the good sense evident in her conversation, a gift that gave me a space, at least a mental space, where I could survive. A gift from a woman abandoned and alone, a volunteer willing to donate her free time, living in an empty but not unwelcoming apartment, sad but strong enough to offer me the first help I needed to set about reconstructing myself.

Around dawn I felt the mattress move. I remained quiet, just as I would do in response to a slight earth tremor. The guest room, decorated with surplus objects taken from other rooms, echoed the creaking bed as Helga got up. I opened my eyes and saw her bending down to retrieve the clothes from the floor. She quickly arranged my things on a chair. Then she picked up hers and pressed them against her naked body, which I saw differently from the way I'd seen it earlier. Isolated from sexual desire, nudes always evoke, somehow, the frigidity of forensic anatomy. Everything on her jiggled, breasts and buttocks, flaccid thighs and forearms, disheveled hair. There was nothing ugly or disagreeable about her, but something inside me felt embarrassed, almost as if I were forced to feel that way. I had fucked an older German woman. A wave of shame I couldn't dodge broke over me. If I analyzed my feelings, nothing was very clear, but my brain was organizing an intellectual and aesthetic defense, all iron barriers and unsentimental barricades.

I started laughing silently. I assessed myself from outside, through the eyes of my friends and acquaintances, and the conclusion was hideous. I looked at myself the way someone on the comfortable side of the television set would look at me. Everything, I thought, smelled like semen and bodily fluids, which enhanced the scene's grotesque and sordid aspects. For a few minutes before falling back to sleep, I transformed myself into a disdain-manufacturing machine. I heard from far off the sound of Helga's footsteps entering her bedroom, then a long pee into what was apparently an amplified toilet. More recoiling, more manufactured ignominy. When she pulled the flush chain, I seemed to pull another chain and send that misunderstanding, which I was blowing out of all proportion, to the sewer. I'm pathetic, I told myself by way of consolation, and went back to snoring.

When I woke up again, I lay still for a while, interpreting the sounds. All I could hear was the agitation in the street. The open jar of hand lotion was on the night table. I was afraid to go out into the hall and encounter the dragon I'd been imagining. I didn't want to see Helga, I didn't want conversation. Maybe she'd try to kiss me or stroke my hand. She might even embrace me or expect to make love again. I thought about breaking into a run and escaping from the apartment, but I wasn't sure I could find the door, and I thought it would be terrible to make Helga chase me down the hall and around the furniture in the living room. I'd scream, like a coward in a castle full of ghosts.

Naked, I stuck my head out the bedroom door and called her. Helga? But nobody answered. I opened the door all the way and walked down the short hall toward the other bedroom without turning around. She was probably asleep. Silence reigned in the apartment, except for the song of a canary I eventually discovered in a birdcage in the kitchen. I went naked into the living room, looked for my overcoat, found it, pulled out my brand-new cell phone, connected to the Internet, and left the phone on an arm of the sofa. There was a note on the kitchen table. Call me if you need anything, I have work to do. Helga had written down the number of her own cell phone and ended with a quick signature, indecipherable except for the enormous H, like scaffolding in front of a collapsed edifice of letters. Then she'd added the word *Kaffee,* with an arrow pointing to the coffeemaker and the clean cup she'd set out for me, and the word *Plätzchen,* with another arrow aimed at a little plate of cookies.

I went back to my room, stepped into the shower, and let the water run over my face. Although the scent of the shower gel was too intense for my liking, I soaped my entire body with it to erase the traces of the previous night. The water poured down, I scrubbed away, and with each stroke Helga's smell—or rather, the scent of her discreet perfume—grew fainter. I dressed quickly. The coins in my pants pockets jingled. I nosed around the place a bit while eating the cookies. I'm always fascinated by coffeemakers, which tend to be examples of the triumph of practical design. Society was advancing, stride after stride, incapable of resolving essential problems, not even the very basic ones, nor those that had to do with human character and its defects, but nevertheless adept at resolving ordinary, minor battles hygienically and precisely, for example, by producing beautiful, gleaming coffeemakers and citrus juicers like Helga's. I paused for a moment in front of every electrical appliance. Then I looked at the pictures in the living room, which had attracted my attention the previous night. Next to the lamp was a postcard with a reproduction of Munch's *Madonna,* and I felt like that monstrous infant in the corner of the painting, a fetal Baby Jesus, gazing neurotically at the ethereal beauty of his mother.

There were various art books on the shelves, too well arranged to be much consulted. There were also novels, well-thumbed hardbacks with warped covers. Almost all the books were in German, except for some volumes on Goya and Velázquez, whose spines I stroked with patriotic complicity. The cat, Fassbinder, looked at me from the sofa, thoroughly indifferent as long as I didn't imperil his repose. I didn't want to spend too much time on the photographs of people I figured must have been her children or grandchildren, in the affected poses family photos encourage. There was a faded picture of a woman in her thirties with two children, both about ten years old, both blond and beautiful. The woman was Helga when she was my age, attractive, resolute, smiling uncomfortably at the camera. If, in another life, that had been a photograph of my wife and children, I wouldn't have minded. Maybe it was the photo she thought of as looking most like herself, before she was changed by the passage of time into someone who was no longer her at all.

I was on the point of leaving, I had my overcoat on, and I picked up my cell phone, now sufficiently charged to turn on. I went back to the kitchen to get her note. It seemed like bad manners on my part to leave the offer of her phone number, along with the possibility of seeing each other again, on the counter with the crumbs from the whole-grain, high-fiber cookies, which had performed intestinal magic and caused a final stop in the bathroom. I didn't want to see her again, that struck me as obvious, but I didn't want to leave signs of ingratitude either. I tried out my new phone's camera with a shot of the coffeemaker and took three more until I got one I liked. On the refrigerator door, two magnets immobilized a postcard, a view of a rocky sea cove with several buildings

MALLORCA

on the slopes above it. I pulled the card off the fridge to look at the back, but there was no writing except for the printed information that the picture showed a nameless cove on the Mediterranean coast of Mallorca. I took a photo of the card too. And I went back to the living room to do the same thing with the picture of the fifteen-year-old Helga. It seemed like a nice souvenir.

On leaving the apartment I encountered an older married couple, who greeted me with suspicion and gangrenous smiles. Although I ventured a courteous nod in their direction, I preferred to descend the stairs with a certain haste. The apartment was on the third floor, the staircase was enormous, and the door of the building glazed. Out on the street, I felt liberated and sad. Marta made her presence felt again, because calls from her had accumulated on my phone, along with a message: please call me. I didn't want her to worry about me, and so I thought I'd call her back. There were also two messages from my friend Carlos, who told me she'd called him, asking about me. Another missed call was from my mother and maybe had nothing to do with the breakup. Maybe. The thought of my mother made me think of Helga. But they weren't the same type of woman. My mother was older. I had four sisters who were making her older and who were themselves much older than me, in age and in their way of life. My oldest sister was eighteen when I was born, and the youngest of the four was ten. As a child I was a toy in their hands and an inopportune accident who grew up with five mothers and a father who died very early, leaving me orphaned of men I could imitate or turn into models. But Freudian dabblers may stop here. I could never visualize my mother naked and panting as I'd seen Helga in the midst of our nocturnal delights. Maybe that was just an instance of the gross denial all children live in, who can't imagine themselves conceived in turbulent copulation, but rather in a conversation between their future parents while sitting in front of the same boring Sunday afternoon television program every single week of their lives. Helga came across as a more sensual, more modern woman, with the advanced notions that German women have in comparison with their Spanish sisters, who when they get older turn into landscape.

Marta answered immediately, as if she were glued to the phone. In any case, she and her phone were never far apart, for she was one of those people who are always waiting for the call that will change their life. Are you all right? Yes, yes, I'm fine, I'm still here in Munich. You wouldn't answer my calls, I was worried. Sorry, I apologized, it's just that a lot of things have happened. Are you sure you're OK? Marta sounded alarmed. I couldn't hear the Uruguayan singer's guitar or voice in the background. I'm fine, I'm fine, I said reassuringly. I wound up going to the roundtable at the conference and they invited me to participate, and I was pretty good, no kidding. I considered for the first time the possibility that someone with a cell phone had recorded my raging assault on Alex Ripollés, and that the video was now trending on the Internet. Where are you staying? Are you still in the hotel? Marta's anxiety about continuing to supervise my life offended me. No, I stayed with a friend, a German woman I met. I don't know if you remember, but at the presentation—

Helga? The translator? Marta's powers of detection took me by surprise, and so I made up a girl, a sweet young university student who'd offered to let me stay in her house because her parents were on a trip. I told this story without details, but it didn't receive the jealous response I'd expected from Marta, who said, when are you coming back? She had a great ability to change the subject when the current turned against her. Soon, I don't know, it's pretty nice here. By which I meant to include my liaison with the German girl. I added something about wanting to spend a few more days in Munich, but then I explained that my phone battery was almost completely down and said we'd talk after I got back.

This suspended conversation with Marta left me stupidly satisfied. Then, when it dawned on me that the lie about my new romance was having a greater effect on my self-esteem than on her, I felt despondent. Marta was musically happy, back with her old love, and she just didn't want me to suffer, that was all she cared about. This desire to free herself from guilt resulted in the written message I got an instant later: I have the feeling I've done great harm to the person in my life I least wanted to hurt. To which I had to make some reply, and so I did, but hastily and indelicately. These condensed and urgent messages made me yearn for the days when epistolary exchanges involved sealed envelopes and liveried messengers, waiting for a reply. Not to worry, I wrote, these things happen. Who was I trying to fool with the fake indifference? And anyway, I urgently needed to put my affairs in order, change my clothes, recover my suitcase, and book my return flight. Or I could rent a car and drive back to Madrid, stopping in lovely places along the way. What's between Munich and Madrid?

I asked myself in geographical anticipation. But I didn't have enough money for such unhurried pleasures; the purchase of the cell phone had exhausted my financial resources.

The sun was shining, and the snow crackled as it thawed. I didn't recognize the neighborhood or the street names and so had no reference points to help me figure out my location and the way back to the InterContinental or the convention center. I saw a streetcar stop, but the sign that showed the route was incomprehensible. Taking a taxi was a luxury I couldn't indulge in, and after walking for a while on some not very charming residential streets, I began to think of myself as completely lost. A young man directed me to the nearest subway station. I remembered the name of the stop next to the hotel, Rosenheimer, and I found it on the map next to the ticket window. The train was clean and silent at that midmorning hour, and I was a recently showered wreck. One more Spanish immigrant in search of a promising future far from the tragedies of his country.

I walked into the hotel and reclaimed my suitcase while the desk clerk gave me a suspicious look. The said look became an uneasy warning when he saw me try to open the door to the computer room, where I wanted to check my e-mail and maybe surf around and find a cheap plane ticket. That's just for guests, he told me. His English was as foreign as my own, but he'd exchanged any possibility of solidarity for a blue jacket and a nameplate. I felt I'd been driven out of Paradise, which in this case was the hotel. My plans, such as they were, had failed catastrophically, and I found myself out on the street, disoriented, with my wheeled suitcase and my dying cell phone. I couldn't very well ask the hotel people to hold my stuff for another few hours. When I wandered into a bike lane, a cyclist almost ran me down and then favored me with an insult in perfectly, admirably enunciated German.

I went to a call center I knew from the day before, when I'd passed it during my aimless wanderings. They assigned me a cubicle, where I started recharging my cell phone and logged on to the Web. Then I started to check my e-mail, but without much enthusiasm. I had a concise message from Carlos that said Marta told me, we have to talk, when are you coming back? Big hug. Carlos was my friend, but Marta always had great trust in him. Instead of writing, I called his Skype number. He was in his studio. Carlos worked for a landscaping firm headed by a well-known architect. In actual fact, the company was a front for a city councilor who was diverting town planning money to his own account, and the architect, a man in obvious decline, served as the councilor's ally in his corrupt scam. Back in the days when Carlos's professional prospects, like mine, were fast deteriorating, his very well-connected parents had found this job opportunity for him, an indecent proposal hidden under an umbrella of prestige, and he hadn't let it pass. He hated to earn money that way, but the more romantic options, such as mine—working for air—had to be ruled out, especially since he was hoping to adopt his first child.

What's happening? Where are you? He kept looking around as he asked these questions. He didn't like taking personal calls at his office. The thing is, I've got the boss's goddamn kid here, they left him with me and I'm supposed to entertain him, and he showed me the child, who was at a nearby computer. Carlos's seventy-year-old boss had married a very young architect, and they had a four-year-old boy. It was pretty ridiculous to see that old guy exposed to the vicissitudes of a young love and exhausted by the difficulties of raising his young son, apparently an unbearable brat they often dropped off at the studio, where the employees were forced to distract him with little computer games and cater to his every whim as though they were operating a one-child nursery school, except that the nursery school belonged to the child in question. He's one of those older men who marry their widow, Carlos used to say about his boss. I'm still in Munich, I said, starting to explain. There was a roundtable at the conference yesterday, Alex Ripollés and I were on it, and I whacked him a couple of times and threw him off his chair. I'm sure the video's already on YouTube. Did you know that Alex Ripollés's name is pronounced Alex Gilipollez in German? What the fuck does that mean? Carlos asked, sounding more alarmed than amused. Look, Beto, I can't talk here, but Marta told me what happened. You're screwed and I'm sorry, man. No, no, don't worry about me, I interrupted him. I felt like staying here a little longer anyway. Don't blame yourself, he admonished me. I know how you are. Don't go around feeling guilty because it's all your fault.

No, don't worry, I'm all right. I even got laid last night. I fucked a girl and spent the night at her house. Well, actually, not a girl, an older woman. A lot older. Yes, a German. A very German lady who lives in Munich. You can't imagine the spectacle. Incredible. I was drunk, obviously, and I wound up at her place. Man, you should have seen me when I saw her naked, with her tits hanging down to her navel and that potbelly older women have. Fucking scary. And there I was, giving my all. At that moment, the boy's little head appeared behind Carlos. The kid looked interested, and how, in my story. Who said that the only things capable of capturing the attention of today's children were video games? I asked Carlos, gesturing at the little boy. After Carlos relocated him, I embellished my account with juicy details.

Stop, stop, stop, Beto, what the fuck are you talking about? Carlos said, interrupting me in midstream while he turned away and once again placed the boy in front of the other computer. When he returned, he spoke in whispers. Are you sure you're all right? Why don't you come home soon? I calmed down and tried to find words that would make him stop worrying about me. I'm all right, totally screwed, but getting used to the idea. Used to the idea, what an innocuous expression. Whipped and beaten would more exactly describe such a state. Marta went back to the Uruguayan guy, the singer, you remember him? Actually, I should have suspected it wasn't over. Marta doesn't like losing at anything, including her past, and this was a score she had to settle. Do you remember the time you beat her at Risk, that game at your place when you two were fighting for control of South America? You got into a nasty argument that showed you Marta's competitive nature and the hidden rage she feels at the thought of defeat. Where are you going with all this, Beto? No, nowhere, I just wanted you to know I'm fine and last night I got laid, which is what I've been telling you about. First he made sure his boss's kid couldn't hear him, and then he said, laid by who? I was with a lady, I told you, a woman old enough to be your mother, no shit, you should have seen me. But good, uh, I mean, it was kind of scary to wake up and see that lying next to me, but it was also great, I don't know, I'll tell you about it, she was nice. She was like the woman in the Woody Allen bit where a character fucks an old lady and says she's eighty-one but very well preserved, you should have seen her, she didn't look a day over eighty.

Carlos smiled, convinced that I was making up a good part—but not all—of my story. She saved my ass last night, I admitted, because I was dead tired with nowhere to go, but this morning I'm practically puking, I swear. I did it with an old lady, Carlos, it's amazing, man, I'm just bowled over. But is she with you now? Carlos asked. Yeah, you bet your ass she is, and I'm going to move in with her, I'm going to introduce her to my mother, they're the same age. Come on, Beto, stop all this silly shit. How are you? I'm sure you're walking around all miserable and fucked-up. Come back to Madrid, come on, you can stay with us a few days until you and Marta decide about the apartment. Instead of having a soothing effect, all his advice and worry just aggravated me, I couldn't stand it, I preferred my cruel jokes about Helga and my headlong flight. You have to come back to Madrid, Carlos insisted, I'll tell Sonia you're staying here for a few days and that'll be that. Carlos and his wife were always in harmony. I should have followed their example when Marta and I began to sing from different scores.

I felt enormous self-loathing for not having anticipated the breakup with Marta, for having been incapable of hearing the music of her thoughts until someone else's orchestra came along and blasted the notes in my face. For having needed one more conversation (that one more conversation's always one too many). And self-loathing for the way I was talking about Helga, trying to get the scene off my chest, relating it to Carlos like a comic episode or something out of Dante. We didn't talk much longer. Before we said good-bye, I had to listen to Carlos tell me that sooner or later everything would turn out all right between Marta and me, I'd see, everything, and I went back to feeling furious. I was going to have to tell everybody about Marta, to give my mother and my sisters the news about Marta. The news about Marta. I foresaw the general disappointment, the empty solace. The news about Marta.

I surfed the Web in search of plane tickets at bargain prices. The cheapest flight departed in two days, Munich–Madrid. The repeated letter M reminded me of Marta. I went through all the preliminaries to buy a ticket on the cheap flight, but the payment page rejected my credit card three times. It was a biblical moment in my banking history, and very humiliating. My funds had dwindled to such a point. I looked at my brand-new cell phone, my last luxury for a long time. I looked for cheap hotels in Munich, but I got bored with the reviews of guests eager to share their experiences. I noted down a few addresses, and through the telepathy of online advertising, every webpage I opened had ads offering me flights between Munich and Madrid. I felt spied on and thought I'd best log off. I saw that my phone had gathered enough strength to last at least until after lunch. The call center was unlovely—lots of cheap wood—and its smell was starting to get to me.

But I couldn't resist looking up the Uruguayan singer on the Internet. The latest news, a recent interview. His webpage offered samples from his new record. His face was on the cover, and the title of the album devastated me: *Spring Returns.* In the depths of my winter, I couldn't help feeling I'd been expelled from spring, and spring was Marta. What was a return for him was a loss for me. Each song got thirty seconds of play time, during which I couldn't stop jumping around. Love lost and regained, past mistakes, soulful lamentations, romantic celebrations. There was a ballad titled "You Never Went Away." I was able to hear only the first verse, but I found the whole song on YouTube, because it was the promotional video for the album. I listened to the thing in its entirety four times, convinced that it had to be dedicated to Marta. There were too many significant coincidences. This was an absurd idea, because the song had surely been written months previously, before their relationship had started up again. But sorrow generates irrational paranoia. Although I had the earbuds plugged into my ears, I realized that I was speaking and shouting over the song. A bastard, that's what you are, a son of a bitch, a third-rate, cheating fraud. The guy in charge of the call center tapped on my cubicle door and asked me to lower my voice. I was no doubt bothering a mother who was talking to her far-off daughter, or a young man reassuring a relative he hadn't seen in years. Was my minor problem serious enough to justify such an uproar?

I decided to get out of there. In the street, I started to cry, and the tears froze on my face. All of a sudden I felt that I had no one. No love, no family, no friends, nothing that really existed in me anymore. Nothing and no one, because no matter how much you're surrounded by people, no one can get inside you. A piercing wind came from the river and blew on my tear ducts. The hand I was carrying my suitcase with froze solid, and I was overcome by a stubborn, transcendental pity. Like a nail, thrust painfully into the inmost part of me. For the first time, I thought about dying. Not a bad solution. The end of all problems. And I'd save myself the return flight, not to mention the night without a hotel. Dying, once and for all, offered only advantages. Any objections?

But I didn't jump off a bridge into the river, nor did I throw myself under the wheels of a streetcar; instead I let the force of inertia tow me down the avenue. My movements were limited by the suitcase, which though not heavy was certainly cumbersome, and I didn't want to set it down and pull it because its little wheels made an outrageous noise on the pavement. A noise that would attract pained looks to the sorry spectacle I presented. I switched the suitcase to my other hand and kept moving. I sat down and caught my breath for a while in a park situated between blocks of buildings at the intersection of Dienerstraße and Schrammerstraße. I stared at the street signs so long I learned to spell the names. The aluminum chairs were bound to one another by a steel cable, probably so that no Spaniard would steal them. I took a picture of the suitcase on the grass. Then I took another shot, a view of the building façades as seen from the park. Saving the photos was like making a map in which I wouldn't feel so lost.

I like gardens, and I like calling them gardens and not green spaces, and I like them because they're an invention of man in alliance with nature. A pact between the territory and its settler, an armistice in the war of domination each conducts against the other. Gardens offer a clear view into man's other dimension. The passion for the useless, for the aesthetic. My thesis director used to maintain that God was the first landscaper in history, and that gardens are our way of trying to recover the lost memory of the Garden of Eden. With every flowerpot, we're aspiring to get back our lost utopia, the dream ruined by so original a punishment.

Once I dragged Marta to the botanical garden in Madrid and showed her the bench where I often used to sit and draw. I enjoyed sketching flowers and other plants in their natural state. But in spite of having been born in Madrid, Marta had never seen the garden. It was the place where I wanted to kiss her for the first time, and so I did. Later, in spite of

the entrance fee the city council charged, we sometimes went back there and walked around, and I'd
make her laugh with my theory about people, namely
that we're nothing but plants that have invented the
fantasy of travel in order to believe ourselves free,
whereas in reality we're anchored to the earth by
a stalk and some invisible roots. Sad flowers bend
down and bow their heads, just as I was doing that
morning.

The night before, I had barely been able to explain
my work to Helga. She told me she'd been with the
landscaping conference for several years, and she volunteered for the film and opera festivals too. You
know talented people, Helga said, justifying herself.
I like to be around them. In her preretirement working life, she explained, she'd been only an administrative assistant in a food import company, and the
rare moments of excitement in her husband's line of
work hadn't done much for her either. Her frustration
had been renewed with her children, who had hum-
drum jobs with international firms. I've always liked
useless jobs, said I. Jobs that offer society something
it doesn't even see. Would this attitude make a mime
out of me yet? When the financial crisis blew up in
Spain, I explained, town and city councils and other
governmental authorities cut every one of our proposals out of their budgets, in a perfect demonstration of
our uselessness, of our lack of essentialness. The exist-
ing gardens had to be maintained, an unnecessary

expenditure the councils couldn't avoid, but they reduced the number of caretakers and cut back on the available resources. The lack of basic necessities was something different. And although from time to time a tree fell or a broken branch crashed down on a man walking in El Retiro park, killing him instantly before the eyes of his small daughters, these events provoked little but rhetorical indignation, which had no echo and nothing to do with landscaping.

I still had my conference credentials in a pocket of my overcoat, and I remembered that there was an area in the convention center where the conference provided free drinks and snack items to its visitors. The center wasn't very far away, and I arrived there resolved to haul my suitcase over its carpets. There were many projects, and now I'd have time to study them. A conference hostess offered to store my suitcase, and as I watched her carry it through a door I felt light and liberated. While nibbling on nuts and fried potatoes and holding a beer in one hand, I sent a message to one of my sisters to let her know that I was staying in Munich a few days longer. It's possible I undervalued my family's capacity for taking me in, for saving me, for serving me as a refuge. But I preferred to postpone the moment when I would open up to my sisters concerning the news about Marta and they would look at me like disapproving tutrixes. Just as everything you have without having won it seems dispensable to you, so too family love, which opens for you like a parachute, never enters into even your most desperate self-rescue plans, though it has the strength of a steel girder and can stop your collapse.

It was the last day of the conference, and posters announced the closing lecture, which was to take place in the main auditorium. When we planned the trip, my only regret was that our limited sojourn in Munich would be too brief for me to attend this talk, which was to be given by the great Japanese landscaper Tetsuo Nashimira. I looked at 3-D models and paged through catalogs, waiting for the time when the talk was scheduled to begin. It didn't take me much effort to understand that I'd been born in the wrong country, a place where landscapers are ignored because the best elements of our discipline have composed themselves; the beauty of our landscape is a gift no one's had to fight for. Often in my conversations with others — Marta, Carlos, friends, collaborators — we'd spoken inconsiderately of Spain. We have to leave, we have to go away, someone said, how are we going to survive here, in the bricklayers' paradise? And yet it turned out that the climate, the customs, a certain level of anarchy, the mutual contempt between the governing and the governed, had caused addiction. No, no, we wouldn't move from there, and the stalk anchoring us to the ground probably wouldn't allow us to anyway. We were additions to the long list of those who were Spaniards in spite of Spain. Perhaps at some point we'd be won over definitively by familiarity, by force of habit, by the sun's punctuality, by the commotion in the streets.

I asked a couple of hostesses for a set of headphones so I could follow the proceedings in English and left my identity card with them in exchange. The conference attendees were arriving in a slow but steady stream that accelerated in the final minutes. Fearful as I was of being expelled for bad behavior—recognized as the violent and rancorous landscaper of the previous evening—I chose a discreet area to sit in. Alex Ripollés entered, surrounded by two or three foreign colleagues, and sat in one of the front rows with his credentials stupidly hanging around his neck. I lowered my head and was delighted when he failed to see me. In a fair fight, he would have beaten me to a pulp. I'd taken advantage of the element of surprise, but now I even thought I could discern traces of gym activity under his shirt. I suspected that Helga was in the auditorium too when I felt the hot breath of guilt on the back of my neck. I didn't want to look around for fear of meeting her, but during the tedious presentations I had a feeling she'd spotted me but was maintaining a defensive distance.

Nashimira's talk focused on a detailed exposition of his latest project, an interior garden inside a center for elderly people with Alzheimer's disease in Osaka. How to make a garden for those who have forgotten all gardens and seem to be insensible to emotions? he wondered aloud. Do we find gardens moving because they bring back memories, feelings, former sensations? He spoke of Alzheimer's disease as a mysterious illness that takes what you've invested in your life without taking your life itself. It reduces us, he said, to the empty vessel of ourselves. The garden he'd designed was a marvel where the four seasons converged. Its glass roof opened it to the sky, and it was a colorful place, filled with flowers and other plants; a little stream crossed by a diminutive bridge humidified the air.

As I looked at the images projected onto the screen, I felt a great urge to go back to work, to do some sketches. This elderly designer was still inventing delights and modestly presenting them. I'd discovered his work during my university days, and in the end he and some other masters had inclined me to the choice of my specialty. I'd listened to some of his recorded lectures, but to hear him now, in person, was to experience something more expressive and more precise. Beauty comes down to appreciation, he concluded. The passage of time is the perfect expression of transience, and it's precisely this fleeting quality that endows each vital stage with significance. The meaning of life is to live according to the meaning of life. I sighed with relief; the man was no disappointment.

After the end of his talk, he generously responded to three or four questions from the audience. Someone asked him what were, in his opinion, the most beautiful gardens in the world, and he hesitated for a long moment. Then he said, the Great Barrier Reef, and added, with an enormous smile, I'd like very much to congratulate the landscape architect who designed it. The conference director initiated the general applause, and then asked for silence so he could read the list of the prizewinners in the various competitions. For a second, I succumbed to the ambition to win. After my behavior at the roundtable, it was more likely that my name had been proscribed.

Not only didn't I win or receive an honorable mention, but also the grand prize in the Future Prospects (*Zukunftsperspektiven*) category was awarded to Alex Ripollés and his Chernobyl Park in Barcelona. I applauded with the rest and listened to his words of gratitude, expressed in perfect English. He ended with a pronouncement that struck me as bombastic: memory is our only resistance against the past. I noticed I was being watched. Maybe some people were fearful that the gardening hooligan I'd turned into would go into action again. After the prizes had all been awarded and the ceremony concluded, the winners gathered on the stage and had their pictures taken with Nashimira. Alex Ripollés put his arm around Nashimira's shoulders, and they both smiled at the camera. I felt jealous. I turned in Helga's direction and considered whether to approach her and say hello. She was surrounded by several women her age, all of whom looked elderly next to her. Well, your

friend won in the end, she said. Yes, Alex Gilipollez, I answered. Thanks for breakfast, I added, but
what I really wanted to thank her for was her tact-
fulness in making sure we didn't wake up together.
Mornings are always hard, she said. I smiled and
nodded. What did you think about our speaker? she
asked. I'd never heard of him, but they tell me he's a
genius. He is, I answered, he's one of my idols. Actually, I'm pretty much dedicated to copying everything
he does.

Have you settled your plane ticket? When I said
no, she insisted on accompanying me to the conference's administrative offices, which were in a private
area toward the back of the building. She knocked on
the half-open door of an office and spoke to a young
woman in German. The girl listened, shifted her eyes
toward me, and gave me a compassionate smile. Then
she appeared to consent to something and again
looked at me, the passive protagonist of their conversation. Helga asked me to give her my full name. I
felt a little ridiculous reciting my two surnames, as if I
were responding to a teacher.

Looks like you're going to get a break, I'll explain
afterward. She waved good-bye. I went back to the
main area, which was swarming with conference
guests. There were people exchanging business cards,
embraces, some handshakes. Young people with little water bottles and their credentials hanging around
their necks, displayed like Olympic medals. If Alex

Ripollés saw me, he did a very good job of pretending not to and ignoring me. I stopped for a second beside Professor Nashimira, who was examining some of the models in the central exhibit. I'm a great admirer of yours, I told him in English. You are a master. He responded with an almost reverential bow and then said, no master, I'm old. I'm just old. And he shook off all my admiration. Then some of his companions drew him away from me.

I looked at the model's title and specifications, and it was his interior garden project. While walking over to him, I'd seen him resituate a bit of grass carpet and adjust a few other details of the presentation. It was called "Garden of Solitude." *Garten der Einsamkeit.* And when I tried to pronounce the name, the German words Helga had taught me the night before came back to me, came back and excited me a little. There you are, Helga whispered to me one instant later, appearing out of nowhere. She was holding a piece of adhesive notepaper, of a frightful color between lilac and orange. My flight information and flight locator number were written on the paper. Your flight is at ten o'clock tomorrow morning, she said. And, almost as a joke, she stuck the paper to the back of my hand. I looked at the writing impassively. Is your suitcase still at the hotel? No, I said, and I told her where I'd left it, near the building entrance. Then I glanced at the locator code, M4RTA, and after a moment I folded the sticky note in half and slid it into my rear pants pocket. We walked toward the entrance hurriedly, and maybe, like me, she felt embarrassed at our being together and afraid someone, including ourselves, would be able to look at us and tell what had gone on the previous night. She too had a right to be embarrassed, for reasons different from mine, but essentially identical. She was wearing a skirt that came down to below her knees, a long sweater that covered most of her behind, her hair pulled back, and low-heeled shoes that helped her propel herself forward at a torrid pace. I stopped so that she wouldn't feel obligated to accompany me any farther and showed her the place where I'd left my suitcase. I wanted to leave and not to think about what was waiting for me outside, the cold, first of all, and then another day to waste in the city, waiting for my flight tomorrow morning, which would land in Madrid, where I had neither house nor home, no roof, no shelter, where I would be as vulnerable as a man without a country.

The information booth was deserted, no doubt because the girls were attending the final celebration. I waited. The hideous background music accomplished its objective of covering up the silence suspended between Helga and me. It filled the painful vacuum for a moment. Are you listening to this music? I asked her. It's horrible, right? She agreed. It's like what we were talking about yesterday, the smiles, the perfect faces, the molded bodies. Helga didn't say anything, but she understood my reference to a certain conversation we'd had the previous night about all the special offers one received, kindly propositions conveyed with pleasant expressions, pleasant looks, pleasant families, pleasant settings, a free massage that stopped us from observing and recognizing ourselves amid so much perfection. Laminated, decorated places where everything glides along smoothly and the going is never rough and the air is vibrant with romantic, melodic music, as when an airliner's about to land. Vacuums loaded with artificial proposals under skies eternally blue. Buried solitudes that present no danger of reflecting you as a mirror reflects what you are, what you lack, what goes away, what never arrives. Terrifying silences that someone takes it upon himself to fill for us, like a person who whistles to drive away thought. Reality reduced to the affordable, like a panther reduced to a domestic cat.

Helga put on her overcoat and wrapped a delicately knitted scarf around her neck. I don't believe I've thanked you for last night's dinner, I ventured to say. Only for the dinner? she asked jokingly. At last the hostess showed up, and when she saw me, she broke into a run, her high heels making a sexy, musical clatter, and opened the door to the storeroom where my luggage was. Well, I said, but added nothing more, and Helga smiled again. Did you have time to get to know the city a little? Not much, I never use guidebooks when I travel, so I wind up seeing only whatever I happen to come across. Would you like a quick tour? she proposed. I felt an urge to refuse, more out of politeness than because a tour would interfere with any plans I had. I've got my car here, she explained.

As she drove, Helga pointed out several of the city's landmarks. A bridge over the river Isar, the English garden. She said we were going to drive past her favorite islet in the river. She talked to me about the nineteenth-century architectural developments that had enhanced Munich and about its postwar reconstruction. She showed me the towers of the Cathedral of Our Lady, the Frauenkirche, which were visible from many parts of the city because municipal regulations prohibited the building of anything higher. Unlike the four towers of Madrid, which had changed the profile of my city forever and shone like flagpoles flying the invisible banner of corruption. When we wanted to build our house in Mallorca, my husband had to grease certain palms too, Helga said by way of consolation. Next we saw the Isartor, one of Munich's medieval gates, followed by the Haus der Kunst, with its massive stone pillars, its abiding solidity, and then the BMW tower, the train station, and a long concatenation of construction sites, some of them old buildings, some of them new additions. She told me anecdotes about Bavarians and offered some samples of their dialect. They call Munich Minga, which is the Spanish word for prick, a detail that very much amused Alex Ripollés when I mentioned it to him.

Then we went back to the city center, left the car in an enormous parking lot, and walked back to Marienplatz. At every step along the way, she pointed out some representative building and gave me a quick summary of its architecture and history. Some classic buildings had grown together with modern glass structures in a combination of time periods. Old things seem more beautiful to us because they've been there longer, I thought. Helga revealed that she'd prepared excursions around the city for people attending the various conferences she volunteered with, and that her collaborations almost always included a walking tour. It's a pleasure to discover your city again through visitors' eyes, she told me. The façade of a nearby building announced an exhibition of works by Otto Dix. I love Otto Dix, I said. Do you want to go in?

It was a small exhibition, about twenty oil paintings, preceded by an anteroom with some dramatic drawings from the period between the world wars, sketches marking out the path that would lead to Picasso's *Guernica*. The oils presented enigmatic faces and some of the pinnacles of Dix's art; the female presences in them were frightened, imperfect, spent, and fragile. The nude red-haired woman protecting her stomach and her chest, her arms covering her bulky, fallen breasts; the rather grotesque pregnant woman hiding her face by turning her head away from the viewer; the famous painting of another redhead, an extremely thin woman with a conspicuous nose and

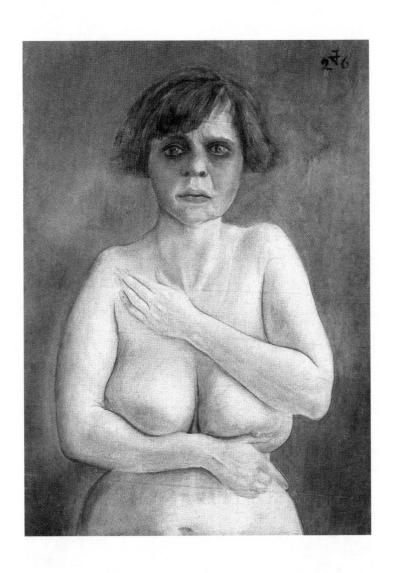

striking eyes; the nude little girl with the red bow in her hair and the delicate veins showing through her skin; older and exhausted women. Dix's work was the most elaborate expression of what the Nazis considered *Entartete Kunst*, Degenerate Art. But what was degenerate was his way of looking, not his painting; his rejection of the cruelty of the real in a dream of reaching purity and perfection.

They're disgusting, Helga said. I don't know, I replied, I'm not so sure. The impression the paintings made was so strong that even the face of the museum guard at the exit, who waved good-bye to us as we left, looked as though it had been painted by Dix. We decided to have some tea in a glass-walled café very near St. Michael's church, which she obliged me to go into in spite of my lazy attempt to avoid it. All churches are the same, I ventured to say. Oh, come on, that's like saying all asses are the same. All right, you've got me there.

As always happens, our tour of the city had been a tour of ourselves. Every now and then, she'd say something like that's where I signed my divorce papers, or one of my children lives in this neighborhood now, or a friend of mine works for that company. I'd point out something noteworthy, a building, a clock, and at the same time, inadvertently, give out information about myself, describe my work or my life with Marta. We were talking about buildings, and we'd be talking about ourselves. We'd allude to a neighborhood, and we'd be alluding to ourselves. We'd point to something outside, and we'd be pointing to something within.

We spent a pleasant, talkative few hours. It was only when we stopped for tea that silence fell. Being stationary inhibited us all over again. It forced us into an intimacy we probably found disturbing. There was a moment when she bent down to straighten her shoe and put her hand on my knee for support. I reacted to her gesture with a kind of embarrassment, but when I realized she meant nothing by it, I felt ridiculous.

Then something unexpected happened. The door of the café opened and I saw Helga's face grow tense. Two burly men, each accompanied by a woman, entered the place in the middle of an animated conversation. One of the men, a blond, powerfully built fellow, was laughing, but when he spotted Helga, he broke off and came over to our table. Helga stood up, they exchanged two kisses, and then they immediately started talking. One of the women also came over, and the earlier smiles and kisses were repeated. Helga turned to me. This is Beto, he's Spanish, she said in English, and then added something in German about the conference. The man turned out to be Helga's son, and the woman was his wife. I got to my feet to exchange greetings with them and couldn't help noticing the excessive force the son put into his handshake. Perhaps it was only natural, given his impressive mass—it was like he was looking down at me from the floor above—but my fingers cracked

inside of his like peanut shells. Despite a great urge
to burst into explanations, I restrained myself. The
woman, diverted by the situation, smiled at me cordially, said something like ah, Spanish, and held out a
cold, long-fingered hand.

After a while, they went and sat with their friends
at the other end of the room. Helga and I stayed
where we were, staring grimly at our teacups, afraid
that any movement we made would be misinterpreted
at a distance. Helga shook her head and made a comically tense face. All right, there, you've met my son.
Yes, he's very big for his age, I joked. He almost man-
gled my hand. Seriously? I guess he *is* a pretty strong
guy, she said apologetically. He has bone-crushing
strength, I said. Yes, he was an athlete at the university. Just as I feared, I said, laying on the irony. What's
his sport, Spaniard-tossing? Or maybe he holds the
world record in the number of bones broken by a single handshake. When he shook my hand, didn't you
hear my knuckles cracking? I tried to pick up my tea-
cup while pretending that my right hand had been
rendered useless. Helga burst into laughter at my
jokes and my antics as I launched into a series of
jerky movements, like an animated drawing, trying in
vain to make my crushed hand work. In fact, I said,
I think I could use a ride to the hospital. You won't
have to explain the architecture or anything like that,
just drop me off at the emergency room and let them
X-ray my hand. I may have several broken bones.

From across the café, the son, alerted by his mother's laughter, looked over at us. Our eyes, his and mine, met for an instant, and he smiled the way you smile at a surgeon. Do you think my life's in danger? I asked Helga. I'm lucky he only shook my hand. If he hugs me, you're responsible for pushing my wheelchair. Helga put her hand over her mouth so she could laugh to her heart's content, and when she saw me shake my aching hand and blow on it for relief, a bubble of air escaped her lips. She took a handkerchief out of her pocket and blew her nose, continuing to laugh the whole time. I didn't stop my ridiculous comedy act, because I liked seeing her like that, unable to contain her laughter. The situation helped to relax us and allowed a current of mutual sympathy very like what we'd felt the previous night to flow between us again. There was something free in those guffaws of Helga's. Her son came over to us again and spoke to his mother, handing her two tickets he'd pulled out of his pocket.

Helga turned to ask me a question. He says he's got two tickets for the soccer match today and he can't go. It starts in an hour. Do you feel like going? Helga and her son awaited my reply. Well, I don't like soccer all that much, I said, begging off. But I thought you'd want to see the stadium—I remember you talked about its architecture when we drove in from the airport. Oh, right, I said, without much enthusiasm. Of course. The son handed her the two little tickets, and then he pulled a Bayern Munich team scarf from his pocket and put it around my neck. I thought he was going to strangle me. *Regalo,* gift, he said in Spanish. *Danke,* I replied in German.

Night was falling as we walked back to the parking lot to get the car. I was wearing the soccer scarf around my neck, and Helga suggested we pop into the Max Planck Institute so I could see the wide stairways. After we left there, she took my arm as we walked along. She asked me the name of my hotel. I confessed the truth, namely that I had no hotel. You're not a very practical boy, I'm afraid, she said. I agreed with her assessment. I always let everything resolve itself at the last minute, I said. Or let other people resolve it, she pointed out. Do you want to spend the night at my place? But no vodka this time, she added. We finished the bottle last night.

We walked among the rows of cars in the parking lot. Helga was still holding my arm, and a blonde girl, leaning on a car close to us and checking her cell phone while she waited for someone, gave us an intense look. I felt an attack of modesty and unthinkingly detached my arm from Helga's and moved a little away from her, and my withdrawal made her feel rejected.

Right, she said a second later. We can't have the girl thinking there's something between us, thinking you're out with an old woman. She didn't say it like a reproach, but rather like an accurate analysis of my reaction. No, no, it wasn't that, I apologized, but we continued on to the car in wounded silence. I myself couldn't understand my attraction to her, or the chain of events that had led to my consenting to spend another night in her apartment, or for that matter the shame I felt at what others would say or think, the embarrassment irrepressibly growing inside me.

In the car, after starting the engine, Helga turned to me. Look, she said, if you really think I'm trying to get in a relationship with you, you're mistaken. As far as I'm concerned, it's ridiculous, I don't have any claim on you and I'm not idiotic enough to think you and I could have any kind of future. I look in the mirror every morning, I see me before anybody else does, and I know what I look like and how old I am. And I also know I'm not going to be able to console you for breaking up with your so beautiful girlfriend. I'm past all that sort of thing. Furthermore, I'm glad to be past it, don't think I have any regrets, it causes a lot of suffering and I've suffered enough. Do you understand? Do you understand what I mean? I'm in a different stage of my life now, I don't want complications, I'm too used to being alone and doing what I want when I want how I want, and what I don't want is emotions invading my life, neither emotions nor the people they come with.

There was some anger in this speech, delivered in faltering English; however, the anger wasn't directed at me. I understand perfectly, I said. But there was also a challenge in her words, in her indifference, in her locating herself beyond the arguments of the heart and the questions of attraction. With positively masculine aggressiveness, Helga slammed the car into reverse. I kept my thoughts to myself and didn't have much to say while she drove. Neither of us wanted to worsen a misunderstanding and bring our relationship to a close like the final speeches at a convention of loners. What had happened the night before would remain in the anthology of shocking moments. Or as she said when we stopped at the first red light, to tell the truth, I imagine you'll keep what happened last night in your memory museum, in the horrors of my life section.

It wasn't a horror at all, I thought. An error, maybe, or a terror, which came to the same thing. At that point, I didn't even know what part of my memory it would stay in, not that it mattered very much; past events find accommodation according to the caprices with which memories are molded by their owner. We reached the environs of the Allianz Arena, which from close up was a box in the shape of a cake. Its exterior of plastic panels was lit up with the colors of the local team. By the time we took our seats, the game had already begun, and our surroundings in the stands led Helga and me to talk more about architecture than about soccer. I told her that the plastic material covering the stadium was a polymer called ETFE, ethylene tetrafluoroethylene. Despite how laughable this show of pedantry was, she seemed impressed. Back in my university days, I explained, I had a professor who was obsessed by the works of Herzog and de Meuron. He even suggested that my final thesis project should be on one of their buildings. But I wound up choosing as my theme the removal of the benches from the public squares of Madrid as a way of displacing the beggars to less conspicuous parts of the city. You know, politically committed architecture and all that, I said, raising my voice above the roar of the crowd while she nodded and leaned her ear closer to my mouth.

We followed the match with mutual indifference and slowly but surely regained the closeness we'd lost. When the local team scored a goal, I caught the euphoria of those around me, embraced Helga, and rejoiced like all the other fans. I've always regretted a little my lack of participation in groups or communities or activities enjoyed en masse. The misfortune of the individualist is that you never feel yourself included in the word *all,* in the expression *people.* And suddenly, without any clear idea why, I kissed her on the lips. It was a long, hearty kiss, something I owed her and she accepted with obvious enjoyment, though the looks she got from her compatriots, who were all around us, made her blush.

She found a parking place close to her apartment. The snow had almost disappeared from the sidewalks, but some accumulations remained in recesses and sunless places. The last time it snowed in Madrid, Marta and I went out and took pictures of the Plaza de Cibeles, the Atocha station, and the Queen Sofía Museum. Memories that still rattled around in my brain even as their traces were dissolving in water. There would be no more snowfalls like that one, arranged just for the two of us.

I don't have much to offer you, but I can cook up some pasta, Helga proposed as we were removing our overcoats. I left my suitcase near the apartment door. The cat abandoned his throne in the living room and came to greet us. He rubbed himself against my leg while Helga stroked his face and throat. I followed her into the kitchen, where she began to open cabinets and choose among some neatly ordered glass jars.

Do you like to cook? I never cook, I answered. We can make pesto, if you like that. It's kids' food, I made it for my children and now I make it for my grandchildren, she said, taking a whisk from a drawer. The drawers and cabinet doors in the kitchen were cream-colored with silver-plated fittings, and I got an occasional glimpse of the pots and pans and utensils inside, all practically and accessibly stored. I have a grandson who likes to cook. When he spends the night here, we make an apple cake together. Is he Bonecrusher's son? I asked. No, he's my daughter's, his name is Andreas. Do you like apple cake? Sure. If you want, I'll make a double portion, it's easy to do. She put some water on to boil and then took eggs and flour from a shelf. Helga could operate the whisk and manage the burners at the same time, with the fluidity of those who know how to move in a kitchen. Peel a couple of apples, she told me. And I started peeling two beautiful green apples. Then she showed me how to slice them thin for the cakes. She took out two aluminum molds, poured the cake batter into them, and sprinkled the batter with raisins. She juiced a lemon and buttered the apple slices, distributed them in the molds, and then added the lemon juice, some powdered sugar, a small amount of chopped walnuts, and cinnamon. I remembered that cinnamon was a well-known aphrodisiac but didn't say anything. I stuck a finger into the remains of the powdered sugar and licked it off with great pleasure. My grandson does that too, she remarked.

She put the cakes in the oven and bent down to set it. Her ass was right in front of me, offering itself through her skirt, and I thought we could end up making love amid the spilled flour, like in movies where nobody cleans up the disorder passion leaves behind. The ceremony of cooking for someone else is always an erotic rite, a rite of seduction. After more than half an hour, I helped her set the table in the living room. Do you want to put on some music? she asked, pointing to some CDs on a shelf. I don't feel like listening to music, I said, and then I described my visit to the call center and listening to the Uruguayan singer's song. *Vuelve el amor, Love Returns,* that's the title of his new record, I informed her. No, no, wait, it's *Vuelve la primavera, Spring Returns.* I guess now he's the stupid romantic and I have to become the cynic. Those are the rules of the game. Helga shook her head, as if I were beyond help.

The moment I took my first bite of apple cake, I wanted to go to bed with Helga again. She offered me some ice cream to put on top, but I refused. The cake was still very hot. We should let it cool off, Helga suggested, but gluttony's always in a hurry. We talked, not for the first time, about my plans for the future, about how I intended to go about moving out of my former apartment and finding a new one. I was thinking I'd give up my work too and find a job that would provide me with sufficient income to live on. It was time for me to stop fooling myself, time to put an end to my architectural career. Hearing me say I planned to give up landscaping made Helga sad. Yes, I joked, it's too complicated to earn your living as a *Landschaftsarchitekt.* I admitted that I didn't have Nashimira's talent. And Spain isn't zen, I said; it's chaos.

I have to tell you, Helga said, I've always hated those sand gardens with the little stones, those Japanese rock gardens people put on their desks. My husband had one in his office to help him relax. When he was nervous, he'd grab the little rake and play with it while he talked on the telephone. I'd be waiting for him to finish so we could go out to lunch together—this was back in the days when I used to meet him at his work—and I'd feel like knocking the whole thing over with one swipe. Sometimes I think I'd like to go into industrial design, I confessed. I may have chosen the wrong career. It seems to me you can contribute more to the landscape by making ashtrays or coffeemakers. I think landscape work's not so much garden creation or urban development as designing people's couches or computers or televisions, which they spend their lives in front of.

But doesn't all this perfection bother you? Helga asked. Don't you have the feeling that everything's too perfect these days? There's something phony in every product. Knives have to look like they don't cut, frying pans have to be decorative objects, nothing can have any rough edges, and then people come into contact with reality and feel defenseless. I agreed with her, but I pointed out that when all was said and done, it was people who had made themselves like that. Of course, she said, all you have to do is look at women who have cosmetic surgery. You'd think mannequins in shop windows were fashioned so they'd look like women, not so women would end up looking like them. I smiled. Yes, people are stupid, I said. No, she disagreed, they're not stupid, the thing is they're afraid. But that's because old age really is a horror, she went on. Decay frightens us, don't forget that. We try to postpone our decline as long as we can, but without much success. Mirrors and I have been enemies for a long time now. But, I replied, maybe the problem is we're not prepared to look in the mirror, we've spent too much time refusing to do that, and if we'd admit that we're simply passing through the stages of life, it wouldn't seem like such a problem. That's very easy to say, said Helga, but try living it. I can assure you that no matter how resigned you are to the idea of growing old, when it actually happens it's a tragedy. You can't go up the stairs, you can't drive, and one day you can't even read. I imagine you keep up the fantasy of winning some younger person's heart and prolonging your splendor, but the end always comes to meet you.

So that was Helga's explanation for what had happened the previous night. According to her, it seemed, Marta's leaving had wounded my pride, and I would have gone to bed with a lamppost just to keep from sleeping alone, just to prove to myself I was still alive. And Helga had acquiesced, succumbing to a fantasy of eternal youth. It was obvious that our behavior afterward—both of us in flight, both rather ashamed—gave no grounds for thinking otherwise. She opened a bottle of white wine and poured out what was our last drink. When my husband and I split up, she said, my first instinct, like yours, was revenge, and it took me some time to realize it wasn't working, to grasp that you can't turn bitterness on and off like a faucet, you have to pour it out until it disappears and leaves room for you to feel again, lets you stop seeing fraud and deception everywhere. That's why I like to spend time with my grandchildren, because they're young, and they embrace life as something new. Whenever we finish doing something, they always ask me, *Und was machen wir jetzt?* And what are we going to do now? And that's the question, that always has to be the question. All right, very good, that's that, and what are we going to do now?

Und was machen wir jetzt? I made a clumsy stab at pronouncing the words. After correcting me twice, Helga shook her head and gave up. I put my wineglass on the low table. She was holding hers with both hands. I started clowning around, imitating the mime trapped inside transparent glass walls. Don't make fun of me, she said, not very seriously. Now I understand why you like that mime routine so much, it's because you think you're trapped too, closed up in a room with glass walls, a room you can't leave. You don't even dare to ask, and what are we going to do now? *Und was machen wir jetzt?* I struck the nonexistent wall hard, and then even harder and more insistently. I kept repeating the question in a loud voice, in my wretched German, and thus reached the climax of my cheap and predictable work of Absurdist Theater.

Helga was sitting on the sofa, laughing that laugh of hers, which she liked to think of as contained but was in fact explosive. I held out both my hands. Put that glass down and come here. She feigned surprise but placed the glass on the table. As soon as she put her hands in mine, I pulled her to her feet and then closer to me. I embraced her and kissed her. Are you crazy? I'm not crazy.

Something I didn't understand at all was driving me. Nevertheless, I let myself go. I gave her a long, placid kiss she gravely accepted. Then she shook her head and said no, that's enough. Why? I asked. After pausing as though to overcome doubts, she said, no, it's not right. I took her in my arms and pulled her up on me so that she was straddling me with one thigh on each side of my body. Do you want me to wind up in the hospital? she asked. If I break my hip, I'm telling you, it's going to be very depressing. She laughed again. And I lugged her to my assigned bedroom. I found Helga beautiful, appealing, fragile, and seductive. I wasn't struggling inside, I felt only excitement at her presence. I kissed her, and when I kissed her, the eyes of other people were no longer on me, their opinions and their conventions didn't count anymore. It didn't bother me to feel the roughness of her lips. Maybe, instead of going crazy, I was going sane.

When I pushed open the door of the guest room, she resisted entering it. No, no, let's go to my room, she said. It's horrible to do it in the bed my grandchildren sleep in. I realized her sense of guilt was greater than mine. That second night was less given over to blind exploration; its hallmark was unequivocal desire, not prefabricated and not drenched in alcohol. Helga's bedroom was a less accidental setting than the guest room. Some photographs of her grandchildren and several big novels in hardback, a sign of many nights spent alone in her bed. When we took off our clothes, I noticed that her underwear was nicer, choicer than what she'd been wearing the night before. That could have been just a coincidence, or maybe an intelligent woman's precaution.

I had no memorable dreams, nor did Marta reappear in my fantasies. Helga fell asleep with her hand on my stomach, and it didn't bother me that she kept it there a long time. In the morning, I had to wake her up. I was afraid of missing my plane, but at the same time I didn't want to sound as though I was in an urgent hurry to disappear. She leapt out of bed and ran into the shower so fast that I suspected she didn't want to be seen in the brightening light of day. Nevertheless, I followed her into the shower, and we soaped each other while I got aroused again and she put up with it.

She refused to call a taxi and insisted on driving me to the airport. She dressed in a hurry and then made coffee, while I got some clean clothes out of my suitcase. It was in the entryway and I had to walk over to it naked, not that I cared. The suitcase and the cat were the two mute witnesses to this spectacle. I stroked Fassbinder's head. What do you think, *mein Freund*? I whispered to him. I've always considered cats aloof, disdainful animals, but that one appeared to grant me the privilege of his curiosity.

We didn't talk much in the car. Still half asleep, we stared at the road ahead, leading us out of the city. The airport wasn't far, and there wasn't much traffic so early on a gray, rainy holiday morning. Neither of us said we'll talk on the phone or see you soon or let's keep in touch. Better if I drop you here, Helga announced decisively, stopping near the entrance to the terminal. I rummaged in my pants pocket, found the note with the locator code for my flight, and read it again. It made me laugh. M4RTA. Can you see this? It looks like they wrote Marta. Helga smiled without much enthusiasm. How stupid of me to show her that trivial detail, which only betrayed my continuing obsession. *Auf Wiedersehen*, I sang out, keeping myself at a cruel distance from the moment, a distance my fun-with-language bit only increased. Have a good trip, she said.

The time had come to decide what form this farewell was going to take. The worst would have been a brief peck on the lips, like an unromantic married couple. A kiss on the cheek seemed like a ridiculous step backward and not a very good idea either. Saying good-bye was complicated because gauging the magnitude of our relationship was complicated. We sat there looking hard at each other, but without frowning. Helga raised her hand and placed her thumb on my lips, pressing them delicately. She made me turn my face away so I'd stop looking at her, and then she said, go on, get out, quick.

I stepped out of the car, took my suitcase from the backseat, and started walking to the entrance. When I turned around, she was still looking at me; she waved briefly, started the car, and left the scene. I breathed easy. I was afraid of leaden farewells, and for a moment I suspected she might stop the car and come and embrace me or burst into tears, which turned out to be a rather arrogant thought on my part. When I couldn't see her car anymore, I felt a pang of wounded pride. What you avoid is what you desire too, I reminded myself by way of consolation. Helga had never lost control of the situation, and however much my preposterous behavior may have surprised her, I'd never had the feeling I was in charge. I remembered the first night in the restaurant, when she told me Marta's real problem was that she was afraid of death. You start to be at ease with yourself, she said, when you start to lose your fear of death. Maybe this attitude of Helga's also meant she wasn't afraid of farewells, those occasional deaths that mark the whole course of our lives, those little deaths that take place at the end of every meeting.

Alex Ripollés was flying home on the same plane. At first we didn't greet each other, even though we were both hanging around the departure gate. We deliberately responded to different calls to board the plane. But as luck would have it, we found ourselves seated next to each other. He got the window, I got the aisle. We had no choice but to laugh at the coincidence. I beg your pardon again, I'm sorry, I said apologetically. Actually, I had nothing against you, I really didn't. I had just broken up with my girlfriend that morning, and I was completely out of it and acting stupid. Alex looked at me intensely, as though for the first time. You broke up with your girlfriend? That pretty, pretty girl? Yes, I admitted. Well then, I'm sorry, she was really pretty. The first time I saw her, I noticed that right away. Very pretty, like a sculpture. I agreed again, but I was beginning to wonder whether this wasn't some kind of cruel joke. I said, I suppose the strangest thing is that someone like me ever had her for a girlfriend. No, no, I don't mean that, he said, but I remember thinking what a pretty girl, she's one of the prettiest girls I've ever seen in my life. That was about the eighth time he'd repeated that word, and maybe he really did want to humiliate me, despite the friendly expression on his face. So why did you break up? Were you together a long time?

During the flight we also talked about matters other than the details of my breakup with Marta. About our projects, and about my professional future now that I'd decided to give up landscape architecture. I was offered a job in Munich, Alex said, but

I wouldn't like to live there. I don't like the attitude people have, they think they've got it all, they think they own everything. To tell you the truth, I think now is the time when we most need to stay in Spain, well, or in Catalonia, because we're probably going to break away from you in the end, but right now the main thing is to try to do what we have to do in our own country, no matter how terrible the situation may be. I agreed with what he was saying, but I added, as long as we don't have to starve to death. I'm patriotic about my stomach. You know what I think? Alex asked after a while. I think I owe you part of the prize. Actually, I believe they gave it to me because you threw me out of my chair at the round-table. Prizes are always compensation for something. And he pulled the trophy out of his backpack. It was so ugly that we joked for a while about who deserved to keep the trophy in his home, the winner or the loser. To keep this thing on your shelf isn't a prize, it's a punishment, Alex concluded.

I didn't tell Alex anything about my affair with Helga, despite the opportunity the flight presented to fill each other in on our lives. The amazing thing about my German trip is that it ended with this very pleasant conversation. Alex suggested I come and see him in Barcelona someday and gave me his brightly colored business card with his address. Maybe we can work together on some project, he told me. Barcelona was competing to be designated a European

Capital of Culture; Alex's team would be included in the preparations, and that always meant work for several years and a rather larger budget than could be expected from the paltry resources of the ruined city and town councils in Spain.

FEBRUARY

Back in Madrid, I got my stuff out of Marta's apartment. She'd moved in with the Uruguayan singer, but I didn't want to stay there alone after she left. I didn't like the prospect of coming across her personal belongings, forgotten under the bed or in the back of some drawer, and crying like a baby. I preferred to get started with my new life as soon as possible. I settled in at Carlos's place and didn't put much effort into finding an apartment in Madrid.

The day I got everything out of the old apartment I made a drawing of myself in front of my accumulated boxes shortly before two Romanians carried them down to their illegally parked truck. That was the best résumé of my thirty years of life: twenty-two cardboard boxes, an ironing board, a folding bicycle, and a mahogany office chair. Oh, and a suit valet, my sole inheritance from my father, which my mother insisted I should keep even though I never wear suits and never use the little cuff link drawer. Maybe that's what your inheritance from your parents comes down to, experiences that don't fit you, biographies you can't relive.

Helga's parents had bequeathed her a beautiful image of married couples, always happy, together forever. And her hidden sorrow consisted in having been unable to imitate that idealized model. There's no such model in my memory, because my father died before he could leave an imprint on it. His absence was the sign of a void that perhaps, in the final analysis, corresponded to the void inside of me; like my mother, I too formed part of a couple, the part that was chained to an absence.

MARCH

Alex offered me a job in his company, and I ended up moving to Barcelona barely two months after our return from Munich. I met his coworkers in his studio in El Poblenou and set about getting myself up-to-date on their various projects. They gave me my own desk. Every day Alex introduced me to some new person who had dropped by the studio. Actually, the place functioned more like a creative cooperative than a company. And Alex's introductions almost always included a mention of my hourglasses. You have to see his hourglass designs, he'd say. I remembered how Helga, in the intimacy of our second night, had confessed that she hated hourglasses. I detest them, they distress me, they fill me with anxiety and fear. That falling sand cuts you up inside like a knife, she said.

I'd taken a photograph of the plaza in front of the Royal Palace of Madrid with my cell phone the day before I left the city, and sometimes I'd take out my phone and look at that photo. The light had an orange tint, and the palace in the background stood out like a superimposed model. I tried to feel some connection, a particular nostalgia. But as far as I was concerned, Madrid versus Barcelona was a matter of pure indifference, a match between archrivals in a sport that interested me not at all.

APRIL

I met Anabel at work. Her department was accounting, but she had excellent taste in design. She talked fast, and she had a sharp sense of irony. Sometimes she wore a pair of spectacles, which she treated badly: she'd fling them down hard onto a desk, tear them off her face to gesture with them, use them as pointers, and sometimes even draw with them, stabbing at the paper and using the little arms like pencils. Her ideas and corrections almost always resulted in improvements. She knew I was looking for an apartment in the city, my salary wasn't enough for a decent place, and so she offered to share hers with me. Anabel was a lesbian, and she owned an enormous apartment in El Ensanche, which she'd bought in the days when she was earning good money in advertising. She was able to let me have the rear wing of the apartment without either of us causing too much domestic interference with the other. Every now and then she'd hook up with very young, very beautiful girls who'd walk half-naked down the hall and into the kitchen, and

I'd observe them from a distance like a ghost peeping at ideal life but unable to reach out and touch it with his fingertips.

Anabel was critical and categorical. To her, ours was a generation of spoiled children unable to face difficulties, accustomed to twisting all the rights won by our fathers and grandfathers in the sweat of struggle and turning them into inalienable privileges. We didn't want to hear that Europe, to say nothing of Spain, was no longer the center of the world, she told me during office breaks, and now we're going to be slapped into accepting that fact. She'd point at the youngest people in the studio and say, they're all depressed and pessimistic and looking for someone to file suit against for psychological mistreatment. And she'd laugh noisily. They're going to sue Mom and Dad for bringing them into the world, just you wait and see.

One day Anabel admitted that she was a kind of vampire. I am, she told me, a kind of vampire. We were having breakfast together one Sunday morning. She used to steal the international edition of the *New York Times* for me from a luxury hotel a couple of blocks from the apartment, and that day she'd said good-bye to one of her conquests and returned home with pastries and the newspaper, which I was spreading out like a happy blanket. When she made the vampire remark, I let a corner of the paper curl downward and gave her my full attention.

I need beauty and youth to feel alive, she said. She was referring to the girls she'd have brief affairs with and unceremoniously dismiss from the premises after a few weeks had passed; the girls were always full of light and energy, and maybe their relationship with Anabel was part of a journey of self-discovery. I listened to Anabel's growling recitals with some amusement, because she was always brazenly bad-tempered after making love, an attitude she attributed to her masculine side. I have orgasms like a man, she assured me that day. Do you know that sensation of tedium after pleasure, the physiological selfishness that makes you wish the person beside you would disappear after you've been satisfied? You wish they'd leave you in peace, because the chief idea in your mind is not prolonging the relationship but getting back in your coffin until you awaken to a new, different adventure. And then another, and another after that. Well, that's the way I am, a sort of vampire thirsty for young blood. That's what Anabel said, and she didn't sound happy.

MAY

One day when I was sitting by the bay window, I saw one of the girls leave Anabel's bedroom, wearing a short T-shirt. She leaned on the kitchen door to drink from a bottle of water and didn't even notice my presence. When she raised her arm and brought the bottle to her lips, she offered a view of her perfect ass, young and smooth, slender and graceful, like a cat stretching herself. I remember thinking about Helga and her very different nakedness. I heard from Helga twice during those months. The first time was a telephone call I didn't answer. I'd just arrived in Barcelona, and I was in a meeting to discuss the project for which Alex had taken me on board. When Helga called, I was being subjected to the palaver of some pedantic advertising guy, and I didn't call her back. Actually, I only guessed it might be her, because the long and unfamiliar number began with a prefix I didn't recognize: 0044. Before getting on the plane in the Munich airport, I'd thrown away the note with her cell phone number. I'd found it natural to dispose of that little souvenir just then, when I was on the point of returning to Madrid after those strange days. What was I going to do? Call her? I let that piece of paper go with no regrets. You throw away the paper and you throw away the person. As far as I was concerned, Helga stayed in that spotless trash can inside Munich's spotless airport.

No message accompanied the missed call, but at work a few days later, I went over to Alex's desk to discuss something with him. When I saw him at his computer, having a video conference, I apologized and made a gesture that was supposed to mean we'll talk later. No, no, he said, look who's here. You remember her? And he invited me to take a close look at the screen. There was Helga. They'd exchanged addresses, she and Alex, and she'd contacted him to ask how he was doing and to send him the photo of him and Nashimira. Hello, I said. In the box on the screen, Helga's face lit up with a smile. I work with Alex now, I explained. He added some joke I don't remember and went over to another desk for a moment. So you live in Barcelona now? Yes, I said. With a certain shyness, she asked me if everything was all right with me, if I was feeling better. Yes, I replied, and then I asked about her and if her family was all right, her children, her cat. My cat? I'll tell him you inquired about him, she said. Well, I said, you know how much I like cats.

The second night we spent together, Helga's cat had kept jumping on the bed, and even though we threw him off several times, he'd ended up sleeping at our feet. I told Helga a story from when I was ten years old and I'd do my homework with an obese friend who would sometimes invite me to his house for an afternoon snack. My friend, whose name was Osorio, had a very affectionate cat, and he used to spread jam on the tip of his dick, and the cat would happily lick it off. On the two or three occasions when I joined him in his secret pleasure, in his room covered with *Flash Kicker* posters, while his mother listened to the radio in the living room, the cat's tongue caused an instantaneous, pleasurable reaction in me, while the animal licked his lips with decorum. Helga's response to this childish anecdote was obvious horror, which she expressed by putting her head under the sheets and muttering something like, men, good God, what creatures. However, she spoke in German, so I'm not sure what she said.

Our computer conversation ended shortly after my cat remark, when Alex came back to his desk and the three of us performed the long good-bye ritual before hanging up. Do you talk to her often? I asked Alex. Nah, every now and then she sends me a photo or an e-mail. You know, she's one of those divorced older ladies with all the time in the world. Right, I agreed.

JUNE

After that January in Munich, I had a few brief flings with girls who always wound up getting annoyed by my guarded attitude. My detachment was absolute, and soon I'd be telling them lies so as not to prolong something that had no future anyway. I preferred going to a movie by myself or just staying home, even though it wasn't unusual to hear my roommate making love with some young girl, one of her conquests, and then a little while later I'd hear her again, disillusioned and growling.

I established a kind of routine with a couple of girls, nothing I took seriously, and nothing they considered very significant either, except for when they felt wounded by my total lack of commitment. One of them used that very expression, lack of commitment. Her name was Noemí, and I had no desire to contradict her. Maybe it *was* lack of commitment, yes, she was right. By the same token, I could have thrown in her face an accusation of overcommitment. A fault as inconvenient as mine.

Noemí had had her breasts operated on. At her husband's insistence, according to her, after the births of her two children. She was my age, but her life history thus far had been more fraught than mine, subjected to a husband she'd finally separated from a year before. We'd see each other only on the weekends her children spent with their father, and I think my relationship with her was based on a certain spite she felt toward her bad-luck marriage. Her tits were firm and round at all hours. One day I thought I'd much rather be cupping Helga's fallen breasts in my hands and returning them to their original height and savoring the feel of real flesh. The memory of Helga lasted for a moment, and then I forgot it. In the same way as the tenuous bond between Noemí and me was destined to be forgotten.

The second girl I took up with was named Monica. I behaved so coldly toward her that after making love we could have chilled our beers over my heart. She was younger than me. On one of those furtive nights when we made love, I asked her why she wasn't looking for a steady boyfriend. Monica, I said, why aren't you looking for a steady boyfriend? I have a boyfriend, she replied. We've been together almost a year. We're thinking about moving in together. What about this? I asked her. This is different, she said. I never again aspired to anything more with her than an opportunity to improve my rudimentary Catalan during our brief conversations as we lay there between the damp sheets.

JULY

In the summer I went back to Madrid for a few days, but I discovered that my move to a distant workplace had also put some distance between me and my most intimate circle of friends. The news insisted that the economy was on the rebound, but the youth unemployment rate was stuck at an astonishing level: fully half of the young people in the job market could find no work. Apparently there were many seasonal positions on offer in the tourism and hotel sectors. I thought I would make a good waiter. I thought I'd like to be one of those waiters who memorize the orders of everyone at the table without needing to write them down and who always ask the customers if everything's all right or if they need anything else. One night, joking with Carlos and Sonia, I said I could serve potato omelets and paella in Plaza Mayor. I told them I could be an excellent waiter-landscaper. Later Carlos told me Sonia had found that remark defeatist. I think Beto's very depressed, she'd told my friend.

AUGUST

Carlos and I planned a vacation we didn't go on in the end, because he and Sonia had to travel to Ethiopia in a hurry to collect a little girl they'd been trying to adopt for two years. I wished them good luck and wondered, secretly and inconclusively, if I'd have children one day. To have been a child but to have no children made me the equivalent of a closed railroad track, not that I cared much about that. What worried me more was the persistent suspicion that I'd lost some of my sense of humor, the thought of which did indeed make me feel like an orphan, and sometimes, for no reason—especially if I was visiting my mother, or talking to her on the phone—I'd fall back on jokes, general buffoonery, double entendres. Not only to make her laugh, but also to remind myself that I could. And then I'd remember the times in the course of those two days in Munich when I'd made Helga laugh out loud.

During the summer I kept busy with the last project I intended to prepare for Alex's studio. Commissions had slowed to a thin trickle, and my plan was to quit my job at the end of the year, because the company was going to lay people off anyway, and I wanted to be the first to go; it seemed only just, since I was the newest member of the staff. I tried to make a joke about unemployment one day in conversation with a colleague, a designer, but she'd already received her pink slip and didn't find me funny.

SEPTEMBER

Alex was very interested in my hourglass designs and promised me he would talk to an investor about developing a line of hourglasses—the two or three best models—and offering them for sale. It surprised me that the word for hourglass, in German (*Sanduhr*) as well as Spanish (*reloj de arena*), makes reference to the contents, to the material inside. By contrast, the English word focuses on the transparent glass of the container. *Hourglass* could be translated into Spanish as *hora de vidrio,* glass hour, a fascinating expression. The Italians and Greeks still use a form of the ancient word *klepsydra,* clepsydra, which originally denoted a water clock. In an encyclopedia, I found the first depiction of an hourglass in art. It appears in a fresco by Ambrogio Lorenzetti that dates from around the middle of the fourteenth century. A crowned and upright queen holds an hourglass in her hand as a symbol of the virtue of temperance.

I assembled these pieces of information in my head in connection with some commercial presentation, a

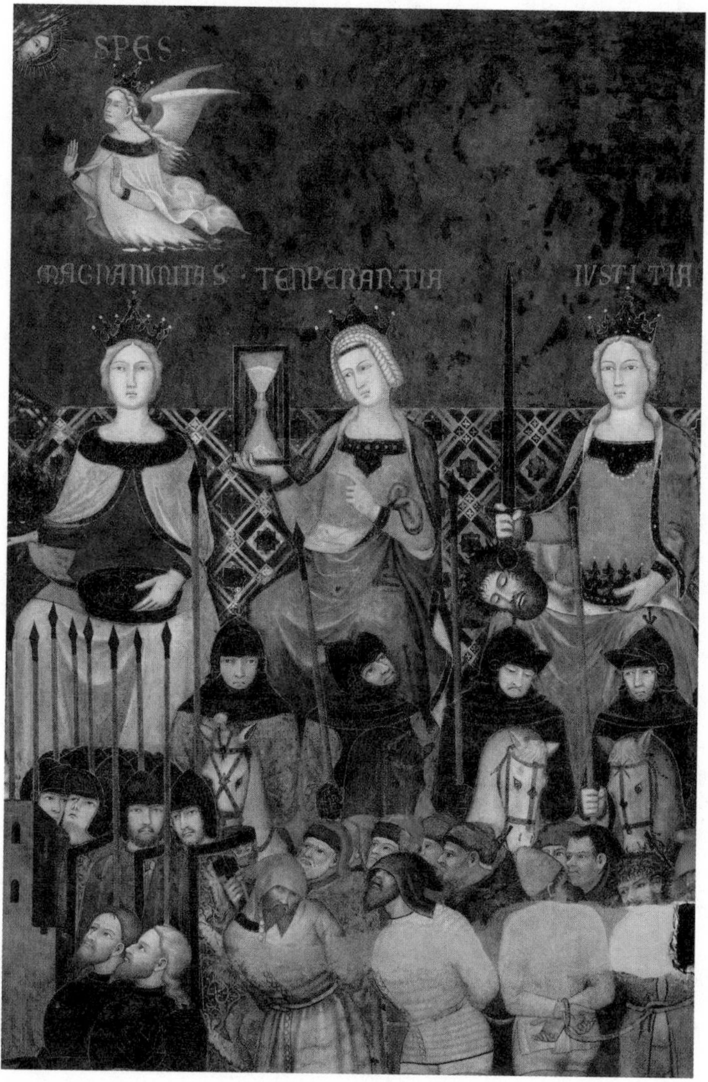
SPES
MAGNANIMITAS
TENPERANTIA
IUSTITIA

process that came to seem as degrading as celebrating the rain because it would wash your car.

I also remembered a remark Helga made once when I was going on about my appreciation for Nashimira and his projects and confessing my obsequious admiration for him. She said—I don't remember her exact words—but something about how Asians considered hurrying bad manners. She also said that was the great difference between us. I think I replied that surely that was a cliché, a stereotype we accepted unquestioningly. When Asians were late for a rendezvous, or when they had only a short time to complete some important assignment, I figured they too hurried like mad.

OCTOBER

In the end, I developed a line of hourglasses. The models I designed represented ornamental objects without very much relevance. My aim was to strip them of the distressing aspect Helga had pointed out when she told me she hated them and surround them instead with a festive aura. Anabel helped me with the prototypes and showed great skill in manual work. I've always known how to use my hands, she told me with a proud and defiant smile. Alex, for his part, proposed an idea. He said we ought to try to come up with a way to associate our hourglasses with cell phones, as mobile apps for decoration or for recreational use, and work to develop them as a business line. *Business line, recreational use,* and *mobile apps* were examples of the professional jargon I was learning to splash around in, like a fish that's taken out of the ocean but grows accustomed to the fish tank in the living room.

NOVEMBER

Everybody was amused by the idea of a mobile app that would be activated by each incoming call and display an hourglass on the screen. As the conversation progressed, the hourglass would empty itself graphically, with a little stream of red sand running through the narrow neck between the upper and lower bulbs. The empty space in the upper bulb would grow larger as the sand ran out of it, and Alex suggested that a message might go there, something like, "are you sure this call is so important?"

Every month, the app would provide the user with a graphic usage summary, in which the sand in the hourglass would be divided into sections whose size would correspond to the amount of time spent in conversation at each of the most frequently used numbers. Anabel proposed selling the idea to a cell phone company. Although it appeared to me that such companies would have little interest in making their customers aware of how much time they'd wasted — since customers' willingness to waste time was the key to the companies' success—I bestirred myself, intending to be useful and to contribute to the profit of those who were now my colleagues. The way to free myself from paralysis led through work, which promised to be pathetic, now and in the foreseeable future. I'd be creating landscapes inside cell phones. Like someone building model sailing ships inside glass bottles.

DECEMBER

I went to Madrid for part of the Christmas holidays. On Christmas Eve I had dinner at Carlos and Sonia's and met their recently adopted daughter. She was five years old, an active and rambunctious child, although both adjectives, which her new parents used to describe her, lacked the requisite intensity. She broke a wide variety of objects in the house, bawled when reprimanded, and calmed down only in front of the TV set. About a minute after I gave her the present I'd brought, a pretty hourglass with multicolored sand that formed delicate designs as it fell, she broke it and scattered the sand over the fish Carlos had cooked for us. She was mistreated in the orphanage, a psychologist had explained to them, and they felt obliged in their turn to explain it to me. Right, and now she's going to get back by mistreating them, I thought wretchedly, unable to ignore the child's unpleasantly dictatorial attitude and her irrepressible violence. I never knew two people so grateful for the tranquilizing invention of the television set.

There were news reports on the TV, the year was being assessed as it approached its end, and everybody talked about the economic crisis. In the year in review, German Chancellor Angela Merkel, with her usual stiffness, offered a cold hand to successive prime ministers of Spain, first Zapatero, his eyebrows arching like a frightened baby's, and then Rajoy, his absence of personality making him look just like a puppet abandoned by his ventriloquist. Both of them seemed to be asking her for more than a handshake; perhaps they wanted her to rock them to sleep, to suckle them at her breasts. But she wasn't the mother they were looking for. I tried to explain this idea to Carlos and Sonia, but they both declared that they didn't want to talk about politics.

At the family meal the following day, my mother and my sisters and I performed the usual gift exchange after they got tired of asking me whether I'd met a girl I liked in Barcelona. Our custom was to organize the gift-giving according to the invisible friend system, where each of us was obligated to give a gift to one of the others, but all presents had to be placed under the Christmas tree without any indication of who the giver was. When my eldest sister opened her present and we saw that it was an electronic book reader, my mother hastened to explain that she'd gotten the idea from my other sisters. I don't understand such things, she said, but they told me you'd like it a lot because you travel so much. My youngest sister protested, don't start, if you explain every gift you lose the invisible friend surprise. The same thing happened every year. When each present was opened, someone would say, if it's not right you can exchange it, or the people in the store told me it comes with a two-year guarantee, or that's very much in fashion now, remarks that would destroy a mystery nobody considered very important anyway.

We opened the rest of the presents with the same inertia. My mother received a tablet computer and protested that it was too difficult for her to operate these modern things. *These modern things* was an expression she'd been using since I was little to refer to each technological novelty. You said the same thing about your cell phone, and look at you now, nobody could possibly get it away from you, my second sister observed, and then opened her own present and feigned enthusiasm when she discovered an electronic picture frame capable of holding up to seventy-five different images in its memory and displaying them at measured intervals. It's fabulous for me, she said, especially since these days we don't have photo albums anymore, and sometimes it makes me sad to see how big the children are getting. My third sister got a cell phone of the very latest generation and reacted with incredulous delight: this thing must have cost seven hundred euros, are you crazy? To which my youngest sister replied that she'd accumulated a great many loyalty points. My youngest sister was great when it came to financial matters. My mother said she had a good eye, but maybe it was a strong stomach. The company she worked for required her to make enormous personal efforts—her expression—and maybe that was why her present was a heart rate and stress monitor, which measured the distance she covered and her blood pressure when she went for her daily hour-long run. One of my other sisters explained to her in detail how to set the monitor and attach it to her forearm. As for me, they gave me clothes. They always give me clothes, because they know I hate to buy clothes for myself, and I like it when what I'm wearing is old and fits my body like a second skin, and my sisters complain that I wear clothes until they fall off me in pieces. The package I got contained two shirts, a sweater, a belt, and a pair of linen trousers for summer.

The end of the year never made me feel particularly sad, unlike the way it affected other people, but I couldn't stop myself from taking stock and trying to put my life in a little better order. For the New Year, I resolved to avoid getting involved in superficial affairs, which in exchange for a brief period of pleasure had done some harm to my partners. I would focus on me, without recourse to other people; I had to heal myself instead of hoping that contact with others would heal me. My only fear was that this change in my habits would drive me to masturbate too much. During my chats with Anabel in her Barcelona apartment, she used to tell me she'd never have children or share her life with anyone. I planned it that way, maybe it'll be sad, but at least I've got things straight, Anabel would say. In life, she declared, you have to get things straight. I didn't have things straight. Maybe it would be a good idea to start getting things straight. First to get things. And then to get them straight.

Marta's shadow kept on hanging over me, and one day during the holidays, in the Fnac store in central Madrid, I saw her from a distance. She was with her Uruguayan singer boyfriend, and I was sure she was pregnant. Carlos told me that was one of my obsessions, but I noticed the way she walked and the protective gesture she made. I slipped away without greeting them, which made me feel like a schoolboy who skips an exam because he hasn't prepared for it conscientiously enough.

And yet, all traces of resentment had evaporated in me. The song that gave its title to the Uruguayan singer's new album was climbing the charts, and instead of making me sad it relaxed me, it took a weight off my shoulders. One day I even caught myself burbling along with the chorus

Love comes back
Spring comes back
The sleepless nights come back
Your whims, my troubles
And our fate
Bound to the blades of a fan

without any clear idea of what all that might mean, especially the line about the fan. But I let it go, I accepted it, though I sensed that this natural reaction of mine, this hankering after no-fault peace, was not generosity but selfishness, self-salvation, a way of distancing myself from other people. In my growing isolation, a sort of mental shipwreck, I hardly saw anyone during the days I spent in Madrid. Upon returning to Barcelona, I realized that I'd lost my locality, because neither there nor in the city where I'd lived all my life was there anything attaching me, anything I was in a hurry to get back to. As far as I was concerned, all the places I knew were deserted islands.

Several weeks previously, Alex and I had arranged a meeting for the morning of December 31 with the directors of a cell phone company's app development division. We wanted to show them my hourglass models. By that point we'd rolled out a collection of a dozen models, which ranged from optical illusions to convoluted mechanisms. Everybody's favorite was an hourglass with a soccer pitch figured in the lower bulb, green grass, white lines, and all. When you turned the glass over, the empty bulb received the sand and formed a new soccer pitch. The time required for the sand to move from one bulb to the other was exactly forty-five minutes. Working out the studies for this design had taken me a good while, and I'd had to change the demonstration model several times, but Alex's delight in the finished product,

Associate it with time
periods everyone knows.
For example: soccer

turn it around and
the field moves to the
other side.
Time required for 'sand'
to run out:

Synchronize it with phone calls.

María R.

09:17

and his faith, were overwhelming. That morning Alex
and I managed to secure a business offer. We agreed
to finish deciding on the details early in the New Year.
But it means quite a lot of money, Alex said, for the
company and for you. We have to celebrate.

Those of us who had come in to work that day—
everybody except those colleagues who'd gone back to
their hometowns or left on vacation—went out for a

celebratory lunch. The talk turned to the New Year's Eve parties everyone was going to that night. They were all immediately scandalized when I admitted I planned to stay home alone and in all likelihood would go to bed before the bells began to chime. To soothe their consciences, and maybe my own discomfort, I wound up accepting an invitation from my housemate to go with her to the home of some women friends who were having a party. There will be heterosexuals there as well, Anabel informed me. All you have to do is bring a bottle of something. Marga, who'd joined the company as an intern, assured me she'd be going too. In several conversations, Alex had insisted to me that Marga liked me; as you've probably noticed, he said, Marga's under your spell, but I avoided Marga because her name was too close to Marta and her eyebrows weren't as special as Marta's, which gave her face a unique quality, a look somewhere between Frida Kahlo and the young Angela Molina.

I left the restaurant fairly loaded and went walking aimlessly around the city until I eventually reached the long avenue called La Rambla. I liked the Rambla, despite the massive tourist presence. One day in La Boqueria market, I'd heard someone complain about the hordes of tourists and get reprimanded by a fruit vendor: the way I see it, the whole population of Barcelona can go fuck themselves, as long as the tourists stay, because they're the ones who leave money here, they're the ones who come and spend. I found this assessment interesting, and it taught me never again to look down on tourists. After all, I wasn't from there either, and what attracted me about that avenue was that nothing like it existed in my hometown. Maybe I knew, like Chekhov, that one's interest in new cities isn't so much in getting to know them as in escaping from those that preceded them.

Lost in thought, I didn't see the street mime approaching me until he launched into an imitation of my pensive expression for the amusement of those who were watching him. I stopped, and the mime did the same. I smiled a smile bright with the Christmas spirit, although I had an obscene urge to slap his face. The mime hid behind my back, and when I turned around to catch him at it, he turned around too, a classic move that made me the laughingstock of the gathering. Then I put the briefcase with my papers down on the ground and started imitating a mime trapped inside transparent walls. Although my level of mimetic skill was pretty pathetic, the mime stopped and watched me and then began to applaud and even gave me a coin he took out of his little cap and told me to be on my way. He looked amused, but he didn't want me to steal his business, and he didn't much like my reaction and what he saw as the cheapening of his craft. Some tourists in his audience applauded me as I walked away.

I saw a blue airport bus picking up passengers in Plaza de Cataluña and headed for the stop. I'd bought a bottle of vodka in the Colmado Quílez, close to our apartment on Calle de Aragón. I was carrying the bottle in my briefcase, which bulged obscenely. Several people I passed looked at the bulge in my briefcase the way they'd look at a hyperexcited penis inside a pair of trousers. I climbed into the bus unhurriedly, chose a seat all the way in the back, and settled in to wait a few minutes before we got under way. The same impulse that had saved me from the mime had made me get on the blue bus and now it took me to the terminals of the Barcelona–El Prat Airport. I looked for a cheap airline that advertised flights to Mallorca. The ad featured a photograph of a well-known model who looked icy and perfect, while the landscape looked fake and cardboard-like. I bought a one-way ticket. There was no line at the check-in counter, but the airline employee told me I couldn't board the plane with that bottle of vodka on me. So I checked it and watched it disappear on the conveyor belt, adorned with the airline's baggage tags, which indicated the liquor's destination. In the newsstand closest to the departure gate, I bought two architecture and design magazines to peruse during the two hours I had to wait until takeoff. I fell asleep about a minute after we left the ground.

In the Son Sant Joan Airport in Palma de Mallorca, I went directly to the taxi stand, where I found several drivers in the midst of an animated discussion. I showed them a photograph on my cell phone and asked if any of them recognized the place in the picture. It was the shot I'd taken of the postcard on Helga's refrigerator, the one showing the unnamed cove. One of the taxi drivers, a bald-headed man, said he recognized it and explained how to get there to the driver whose turn it was. Once we're in the area I'll tell you where to let me off, I said after getting into his cab. I told him I was looking for someone, and I'd stop and ask in some shop. There's not much in the way of shops there, he said; if you want, I could drop you at the tennis club. I told him to do that, but when we arrived night had fallen, and the club looked abandoned and deserted, with two or three skinned tennis balls lying forgotten next to the rusty fence, and so the cabbie took me to a nearby hotel.

I went in, stepped up to the reception desk, and inquired about the hotel's rates. The desk clerk's suspicious look discouraged me from getting a room. I asked her if she knew a German woman named Helga who usually spent the Christmas holidays in this part of the island. The clerk told me she didn't know people with houses in the area, just regular tourists. I'm afraid I can't help you, the girl said apologetically. Undaunted, I asked her about the cove and the houses overlooking it on the postcard, and she was generous in her explanations. She pointed to one end of the cove and said, from this point it's all a cliff, there aren't any houses.

I left the hotel with an uncertain promise to be back. I walked along the street, which was paved but badly lit. There were houses on the mountainside, and if I went all the way to the end of the cove, I figured I could get a more general overview. But I didn't know the exact address of the residence I was looking for, or even what it looked like. There were lights on in some of the houses, and I could see Christmas decorations, but the only sound that broke the silence came from the headstrong waves, which were smashing themselves against the rocks below.

I kept going for a while and then took a road flanked on both sides by pine trees. I came upon a restaurant with an empty swimming pool and beach umbrellas on poles, topped with dried palm leaves. There were also some big, heinously arrogant houses. I remembered what Helga had said about her house, but I was beginning to harbor doubts about whether this really was the place she'd told me about, the cove where she usually went at the end of the year.

I walked back to the main street and saw a water truck parked next to the gate of a large house. The driver had finished making a delivery and was rolling up the thick plastic hose. He was a ruddy-cheeked young man who wore his blond hair cut short. I'm trying to find a German lady, I said. Her house is around here somewhere. When I said the word *lady*, I felt myself blushing slightly. Around here is full of Germans, the kid said, going on with his work. She and her husband are divorced, but she always comes down here alone for New Year's Eve. She lives in

Munich. Helga? the youngster asked immediately, securing the hosepipe to the back of the water tank.

Seized by a not-altogether-rational enthusiasm, I accepted his invitation to climb into his water truck. He could drop me off at Helga's house, he said. Actually it's her husband's house, she doesn't come here much. Are you a relative of hers? Yes, her nephew. She's a really nice lady, it's not easy to find people like that around here, believe me. You gotta watch out with Germans, they're mostly a pain in the ass. Her children come more often. Yes, her son's a big guy, huh? I know him. For a moment I imagined that the young driver had also had an adventure with Helga, that she was a man-eater always setting up "accidental" meetings. The idea terrified and fascinated me at the same time. Then I looked at the driver more carefully, and my idea seemed like a ridiculous fantasy. The kid lacked sufficient imagination to see in Helga anything other than a retired German lady living her golden years.

He left me at the blue wooden gate of a small house. I couldn't find a doorbell of any kind, so I opened the gate, stepped onto the property, and went up to the door. The house faced the sea, and although now I did see a switch that might have been a doorbell, I preferred knocking on the door, which looked like a rear entrance, little used. I could hear sounds and music inside, and I kept knocking and calling until someone came up the stairs.

A German man, one of those reddish German pensioners you find in Mallorca, welcomed me cordially. For a moment I thought he might be Helga's husband. He seemed not altogether sober. There was less than an hour to go before midnight ended the old year and began the new one. When I asked for Helga, the German made a gesture to indicate that I should wait and ran back inside, calling her name. I heard her footsteps coming up the same stairs the man had disappeared down. I stepped back so she couldn't see me until she was standing in the doorway.

Her face changed from a vague smile to genuine surprise. She might have been expecting a neighbor, or maybe even some working person. Never me. I said one word, hello, and her reply was as shy as my greeting. I remembered you always spend New Year's Eve here, I declared, and that was all I said. Do you want to come in? Helga asked. I've got some of my neighbors here. I opened my bag and pulled out the bottle. I brought some vodka, I said. I don't know whether she recognized it as the same Polish vodka we'd drunk that first night in her apartment, the bottle with the little blade of bison grass inside.

There were two German couples of around Helga's age, among them the man who'd opened the door. Besides them, there was an older German lady, sunburned and as red as a lobster. She appeared to be alone and tipsy from the wine. Helga introduced me to the company in German, and I didn't understand very well what she added about me. Maybe she lied to them too, maybe she told them I was a Spanish nephew of hers. I was handed a plate with leftover salmon and salad, they gave me a glass and filled it with white wine, and every time one of them passed me, he or she insisted on clinking glasses and toasting. *Prosit.* The television was on, its sound drowned out by the music on the radio. It was a Spanish TV channel, and at that very moment, the tower clock in Puerta del Sol filled the screen.

I didn't speak very much with anybody, nor did Helga come close to me for a private exchange that might perhaps have made the others curious. Every now and then she helped translate something someone was saying to me and explained what they did or how close their house was to hers. When the bells began to strike midnight, everybody joined in the countdown to the New Year. They should use an hourglass to celebrate the end of the year, right? Helga suggested to me with a smile. The Spanish tradition of eating twelve grapes, one for each stroke — *las doce uvas de la suerte,* the twelve grapes of luck — was ignored, there wasn't a grape in sight, and I couldn't bring myself to ask for any. It was the first December 31 in my life when I didn't eat grapes to welcome the New Year, so I settled for taking twelve sips of wine. I skipped worrying about my future prospects, my *Zukunftsperspektiven,* too. *Ein glückliches neues Jahr,* I repeated with them, while they laughed at my pronunciation. Then they set off firecrackers and a couple of rockets, just as the people in nearby houses were doing.

The farewells began around two in the morning; the lobster lady was the last to go. She'd more or less disintegrated on the sofa, and Helga invited her to stay, but she shook her head and pulled a little flashlight out of her purse and showed us how she was going to find her way home in the dark, like a witch in a fairy tale about to take off on her broom. Helga escorted her up the stairs to the front door while she kept on saying *Nein, nein* to every suggestion that she could sleep in one of the bedrooms in Helga's house.

When Helga came back to the living room, I was out on the deck. From there I had an unobstructed view of the bright stars shining down on the dark and boundless Mediterranean, whose mighty roaring never stopped. The cove, a natural refuge shaped by the wind and the tides, looked like a hand cupped to receive the sea, or like two long arms extended to receive it in a rocky, hospitable embrace. The vodka bottle had remained untouched, so I'd opened it and poured myself a little glass, and Helga filled one for herself and came outside. She and her guests had danced for a while, but I'd turned down their frequent and insistent invitations to join in, preferring to watch them from a certain polite distance. It wasn't my party.

What a pretty spot this is, I said. She confined herself to a few words of agreement and then followed the direction of my gaze. I was walking around in Barcelona this afternoon, and all of a sudden I thought about coming here. It sounded like an unsolicited explanation that didn't make much sense. It's cold, she said, as if she'd rather interrupt me than listen to more self-justifying. She ducked into the living room and came back out with the blanket that had been draped over the armchair. She put the blanket around her shoulders and held out one end to me. It was soft and plush—camel hair, I would have said, if I'd been able to tell the difference between that and any other fabric; it was surely not some low-quality Chinese synthetic. I moved closer to her, each of us clenched a fist around one end of the blanket, and we stood there side by side, fists pressed against chests, clenched hands touching. In German we call this cove *Blitz*. Lightning.

Illustration Credits

DAVID TRUEBA is a film director and screenwriter as well as a novelist. He is the author of *Cuatro amigos*, which sold more than 100,000 copies in Spain, and his English-language debut, *Learning to Lose*, which won Spain's National Critics Prize in 2009. Trueba's latest film, *Living Is Easy with Eyes Closed*, which he wrote and directed, was long-listed for an Academy Award for Best Foreign Film in 2015 and won Goya awards for Best Film, Best Director, and Best Original Screenplay, among others.

JOHN CULLEN is the translator of many books from Spanish, French, German, and Italian, including Philippe Claudel's *Brodeck*, Juli Zeh's *Decompression*, Chantal Thomas's *The Exchange of Princesses*, and Kamel Daoud's *The Meursault Investigation*. He lives in upstate New York.

LEARNING TO LOSE by David Trueba

From one of Spain's most celebrated contemporary writers, a lucid view into the complexities of lives overturned and the capriciousness of modern life

"One part Paul Thomas Anderson's *Magnolia*, one part Paul Haggis' *Crash*, the rest is all David Trueba, modern-day Madrid, and a narrative that pulsates with longing, lust, and simmering rage...Simply masterful." —Joe McGinniss, Jr., author of *The Delivery Man*

COUPLE MECHANICS by Nelly Alard

At once sexy and feminist, this is a story of a woman who decides to fight for her marriage after her husband confesses to an affair with a notable politician.

"Nelly Alard delves into the core of infidelity with wry observation and subtlety. Riveting, beautifully detailed, and totally addictive. You won't be able to put this down." —Tatiana de Rosnay, *New York Times* best-selling author of *Sarah's Key*

ALL DAYS ARE NIGHT by Peter Stamm

A novel about survival, self-reliance, and art, by Peter Stamm, finalist for the 2013 Man Booker International Prize

"A postmodern riff on *The Magic Mountain*... a page-turner." —*The Atlantic*

"*All Days Are Night* air[s] the psychological implications of our beauty obsession and the insidious ways in which it can obscure selfhood." —*New Republic*

Also recommended:

ALL RUSSIANS LOVE BIRCH TREES
by Olga Grjasnowa

An award-winning debut novel about a young immigrant's journey through a multicultural, post-nationalist landscape

"Grjasnowa gives us a fresh, important understanding [of immigration] from the European perspective... [A] touching and thought-provoking debut novel."
—*Library Journal*

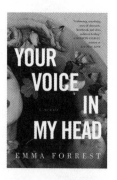

YOUR VOICE IN MY HEAD by Emma Forrest

A stunning memoir that explores the highs and lows of love and the heartbreak of loss

"Emma Forrest is an incredibly gifted writer... I can't remember the last time I ever read such a blistering, transfixing story of obsession, heartbreak, and slow, stubborn healing."
—Elizabeth Gilbert, author of *Eat, Pray, Love*

GALORE by Michael Crummey

A multigenerational epic set in the magical coastal town of Paradise Deep, full of feuds, love, and lore

"Crummey has created an unforgettable place of the imagination. Paradise Deep belongs on the same literary map as Faulkner's Yoknapatawpha and García Márquez's Macondo." —*Boston Globe*